ACKNOWLEDGMENTS

With special thanks to Sonya Haskell,

Gushiba Santhiralingam, Amy Wilkins, and

Tracey Bahadur, instructor extraordinaire of bobbing,

weaving, jabs, hooks, and uppercuts.

Gwyneth and the Thief

❧

CHAPTER ONE

England, 1202

Lady Gwyneth of Haverleigh, fifteen and weary, breathed deeply as she tilted her head and looked up at the sky. Weak wintry morning sunlight shone through the barren branches of the wood. To her right ran the river, swollen with melting snow. To her left a steep slope rose, shielding her from the north wind. Despite that, she shivered and wrapped her cloak more tightly about her before she sat upon a fallen log.

Her dog trotted up to stand beside her, and she reached out to pat his massive dark brown head.

"We'll go back soon, Rufus," she promised. "Just a little while longer."

In truth, she could not and should not linger long here, because she was alone save for her hound, but she needed the peace and quiet, if only for a brief time. It was difficult having everyone in Haverleigh look to her for guidance, as they had since her father had fallen seriously ill. Her mother had died when she was less than two years old, and her elder brother had passed away of a fever five years ago, which meant she was in temporary charge of the estate, although she was only a girl.

Indeed, a year ago, she would not even have been permitted to walk out of her father's castle without an escort. That was when they could still afford to keep a garrison, and before a bad harvest and the cost of equipping her late brother as a knight had depleted their funds. They had used all that remained of their money to pay King John's taxes. When the soldiers of the garrison realized her father could not pay their wages, they had departed.

Her father had never paid much heed to money, as long as Haverleigh provided enough to pay the taxes and allow them to live in some ease. Unlike many a noble, including their neighbor, Baron DeVilliers, the earl of Haverleigh had no lofty, grasping ambitions.

Unfortunately, her father had not foreseen how an illness, a bad harvest, and an increase to their taxes might one day put his family, his estate, and their village in jeopardy. Baron DeVilliers, whose personal greed knew no bounds, had seen an opportunity. Shortly after Gwyneth's father had become sick, the baron had arrived at Haverleigh to offer her both his protection and marriage.

She would rather marry the meanest pauper in London than marry Baron DeVilliers. As for his "protection," he would use that as an excuse to gain control of her family's estate, though her father yet lived.

So now her days were filled with trying to run the estate, and preventing DeVilliers from swooping down like a hawk to snatch it from her.

How she wished her father was better, her brother alive, and her mother, too! Then she would not have this great burden pressing on her day after day, hour after hour. Even now it was tempting to keep on walking through the forest and away from the responsibilities that awaited her back in Haverleigh.

But she could not and would not abandon her father or the people who lived on their estate. She was the earl of Haverleigh's daughter, and she would not shirk her duty. To do otherwise would be dishonorable and disgraceful.

With a low growl, Rufus stiffened and raised his head—a warning that someone was coming.

Gwyneth jumped to her feet, straining to see through the trees, her ears alert for any unusual noise. The unexpected sound of male voices drifted toward her like spirits on the wind.

Who could it be? This was her father's land, and nobody lived near here.

Maybe it was outlaws or poachers. If they were thieves, her fine cloak would be reason enough to attack her.

Her fear building, she tried to whistle for Rufus, but her throat and lips were dry with dread.

"Rufus, come!" she croaked as she began to clamber up the muddy, slippery slope. She grabbed on to roots and rocks, and paid no heed to the mud clinging to her clothes.

Rufus thought this some kind of game. His tail wagged, his eyes gleamed, and he yipped like a puppy as he gleefully followed her.

Once at the top, she threw herself down in the mud behind a fallen tree. Rufus flopped beside her, his tail still wagging, but at least he was mercifully silent.

Peering through the space between the log and the ground, barely breathing, she watched four rough-looking men approach on the path below her. All wore brown tunics, dark woolen breeches, and thick leather boots. Each carried a sword in a scabbard dangling from a belt at his waist. All but the last had another knife stuck through his belt.

The man in front, who looked to be the leader of the small band, was very tall and lean. A long, thin scar curved from the outer edge of his brow to his chin. The two men behind him were heavier, and she could hardly see their faces for the dirt and their long, straggling dark hair. They both carried large leather pouches.

The fourth man brought up the rear. He was more slender than the others and wore no linen shirt beneath his leather tunic, so his muscular arms were bare despite the winter chill.

These men had to be thieves or poachers and were surely very dangerous.

Wishing she had never left the castle, Gwyneth tried to flatten herself even more against the ground.

"We'll rest here," the tall man announced in a harsh, stern voice as he came to a halt where she had been moments ago. He sat down on the fallen log and waited until the others had stopped. "'Ere, give us that pack, Drogo," he said to the biggest of the filthy men. "Time to split the takings."

The burly man handed over a large leather sack. The leader sat it on the ground, and as the others gathered around, he drew some smaller leather purses from it, the kind well-to-do men wore tied to their belts beneath their cloaks.

Gwyneth didn't know anyone wealthy enough to wear such a purse in or around Haverleigh. These men must have come from Salisbury.

The leader eyed the fourth fellow. "We'd 'ave 'ad more if His Highness over there didn't have a soft spot for the ladies."

The two filthy men chuckled in a way that made Gwyneth's blood run cold.

"There were plenty of men's purses to take," the fourth one offered with a shrug. He had a slight accent that made her wonder if he was a Scot.

More surprising, he sounded only a little older than Gwyneth—eighteen, at most—and of a much higher class.

Young in years, perhaps, but old in sin if he was with these others. As for his manner of speech, no one was born a thief.

Rufus whimpered and she quickly put her arm around him to hold him still. Whether any of them was high ranking or not, she was sure they would hurt Rufus if they caught him. As for what they would do to her, she didn't want to think about it.

The leader frowned. "You're lucky you got as many as you did, Gavin, or I wouldn't be in so good a humor."

The young man crossed his arms. "Since I did all the purse cutting and took all the risk, you *should* be happy."

"'Ere, what's this, then? Baby goin' t' cry?"

"I think I should have half, Fulk, not a quarter. While I was cutting purses, you were all sitting in a tavern, well in your cups."

The one called Fulk got to his feet. "Well, ain't you the hoity-toity one? Just 'cause your mam was a Scots lady. Tell us again how she died, eh? And who your father was?"

As the young man scowled, the older one grinned with horrible mockery. "Don't know who he was, do ya? He left her when she got with you, and the rest o' your high and mighty family cast her out like the whore she was. And you think that means you can put on airs, boy?"

"The way I sound has paid for your ale more than once, Fulk. It gets me into places your lot wouldn't dare venture, as you well know."

"And because it does, we protect you—or are you forgettin' that? You ain't been hanged yet, have you?"

"No. But I'm not a little boy needing your protection anymore, either."

"Oh, you're not?" Fulk demanded.

"No. Now, give me my share—the last share you'll ever get because of me—and I'll be on my way."

"Just like that, eh, Gavin? You think you can stand here and tell us you're leaving?"

"Why not? I've repaid anything you ever spent on me for food or rags to wear." Gavin took a step closer. "Surely you don't expect me to be grateful for the way you 'protected' my mother?"

"She needed a man's safeguarding, or she'd have been dead in a fortnight—"

"She needed money, and by the saints, she got it the only way she could," Gavin growled, his accent growing stronger with his rage. "Aye, she might have died all the sooner from a knife or a blow, but you saw to it she lived—and she paid you your share, until she couldn't bear it and ended her miserable life. But by then, I was old enough to steal, so no matter, eh, Fulk?"

Drawing his sword, Fulk glanced at the other two men. "Fine thanks, this, eh? We take the little beggar in, train him proper, and when he starts to pay us back, he tells us he's desertin'. It ain't that easy, Gavin."

The others went to stand behind Fulk, making it three against one.

"I won't turn you in," Gavin retorted even as his hand moved to the hilt of his sword, "if that's what you're worried about, tempting though it may be. Why would I, when I'm as guilty as you?"

"Fer money, or t' save yer own neck."

"I give you my word that I won't."

"As if I'd take your word!"

Gwyneth held her breath as Gavin began to pull his sword from its scabbard.

"If you can't," he said, "it's because I am what you made me. Now, give me my money and let me go. Find another gutter brat to train to be a thief. There are plenty more where I came from."

"But few who sound like right popinjays when they want, or are quick and light on their feet," Fulk retorted. "And we was just going to head to London. That's where the real money is." His sword swayed menacingly. "I really think you ought t' change your mind, me buck. It'd be a pity t' have t' lose a hand or an eye t' learn a lesson."

Gavin took another step forward, his eyes fairly blazing with anger and determination, the way a warrior's would on a battlefield if he faced a detested enemy. "Aye, but I'll fight you if I have to, Fulk."

Fulk put his other hand on the hilt of his sword.

Gwyneth's heartbeat quickened, for a firmer grip surely meant he was preparing to strike.

"So, you want to try me, eh, Gavin?" Fulk jeered. "Think you can beat me, do ya? I warn you—you'll be sorry."

At that, Gavin ran forward and threw his shoulder against Fulk's side. They fell together, Gavin on top. Fulk's sword swung through the air. Gavin rolled out of the way. Panting, he jumped to his feet, while Fulk staggered upright. Then they both crouched, swaying slightly, swords at the ready, circling each other.

"I'm gonna kill you for that," Fulk snarled.

"You can try."

Rufus started to whine.

"*Shhh*, Rufus. *Quiet!*" Gwyneth urged in a whisper, her gaze fixed on the combatants below.

"Drogo, Bert—you'd better help me," Fulk said.

They drew their swords, yet didn't move any closer.

"If you die, Fulk, they won't have to share the take with you, you see," Gavin noted with a sneer.

"And if you die, that's more for us, too," Fulk countered.

Gavin suddenly bent and grabbed a handful of dead leaves and dirt. He threw it at Fulk and caught him square in the face. As Fulk spluttered and stumbled back, Gavin ran forward, raising his sword.

Before Gavin could strike, Fulk recovered and blocked

the blow. The clang of sword on sword seemed to fill the wood as they swung their long, dangerous weapons at each other.

Fulk must have been a soldier, Gwyneth realized. An untrained peasant who tried to use a sword swung it like an ax, expecting the weight of the weapon to do all the work, the way an ax head made chopping easier. A trained soldier knew to use his back as well as his shoulders and arms, to move in one fluid motion—he expected his body to provide the power, not the sword. Waiting, Fulk held his sword directly in front of his chest to protect himself.

Gavin did, too, at first, and he parried Fulk's blows with skill. Soon, though, the point of his weapon hung low, nearly in the mud, as if he was too exhausted to hold it upright. That left his chest unguarded, and she feared the worst until Gavin suddenly rushed forward and lifted his sword directly upward, coming at his enemy from below instead of head on or sideways. His sword slashed Fulk's upraised arm. Fulk shouted a curse and dropped his sword.

She nearly cried out in amazement. Gavin's apparent fatigue had been a feint—a mere deception—and it had worked! Unorthodox it might have been, perhaps even something a knight would consider dishonorable, but it had certainly been effective.

Then one of the men behind Gavin crept toward him. He raised his sword, ready to bring a blow down on Gavin's head.

Gwyneth shrieked and half rose—and Rufus took it as a signal to leap over the log and bound down the slope.

Gasping, terrified that she'd been seen and heard, she threw herself back down behind the log. She stared through the gap, terrified that they would start climbing toward her. Despite that, she had to get Rufus, so she desperately tried to whistle again to call him back, to no avail.

At the sight of the dog bearing down on them, the men froze where they stood, until the one behind Gavin cried, "A hunting hound!"

Taking advantage of the distraction, Fulk rushed at Gavin, catching him off guard, knocking him to the ground, and punching him hard. "That's for thinking you could leave us, boy. I could stick you like a pig, but I won't, because the knight what owns that hunting hound is sure to hang you for trespassin' on his land!"

Gavin didn't respond. He didn't even move, although Rufus ran up to him and started sniffing him.

Meanwhile, the two filthy men grabbed the leather pouch and stuffed the purses in while Fulk grabbed Gavin's sword. Then they fled along the path.

The blood throbbing in her ears, her heart pounding like a minstrel with a drum, Gwyneth waited behind the log for what seemed an eternity, watching Rufus examine and paw the fallen young man. Eventually Rufus sat beside him and looked expectantly up the hill, as if waiting for her to join them.

She wasn't going to move until she was sure those men were really gone.

Finally, when she felt it was safe, she rose. Her legs trembled a little as she brushed the leaves and mud from her cloak and gown.

She didn't want to go near that thief, even if he was unconscious. She only wanted to get Rufus and hurry safely home. Once there, she would send for Thomas the reeve. As her father's representative in the village, he could gather some men and come to get this ruffian. She would also tell him to be on the lookout for the fallen man's comrades.

"Rufus!" she called out as loudly as she dared.

He didn't move. He just sat on his haunches and looked at her.

She didn't want to leave him. Those men might decide to come back for their companion and steal Rufus or hurt him.

"*Rufus!*" she called again, and still he didn't move.

Gavin didn't move, either. Was he dead, or only unconscious? If he wasn't dead and lay out all night, the cold or an untended injury might kill him.

So what if he *did* die? He was a thief, an outlaw—maybe even a murderer—and the punishment for such crimes would be death.

Despite that, a spark of pity kindled in her heart. Given what she had heard of his history, was it any wonder he was a thief? What other alternatives had life offered him but stealing and cutting purses?

She was a Christian, and should be merciful and charitable. If she let him die, his death would be her fault because she had done nothing to prevent it. Of course, she might be saving his life only to send him to a horrible end in a hangman's noose . . . unless he could be made to see the error of his ways, repent, and become something better than a thief.

She couldn't spend any more time dithering. The first thing she must do, she decided, was to see if the young thief was alive or dead.

She made her way carefully down the hillside, trying not to slip. She came to a halt about four feet from where he lay, flat on his back, his arms flung outward as if in surrender. A nasty bruise had formed on his temple, and blood trickled from a gash. His chest rose with his breathing, though, so he was still alive.

She studied his face. It wasn't a bad-looking face, beneath the dirt. He might even be quite handsome. She moved a little closer, noting the angles and planes of his chin and cheekbones, and the excellent teeth beneath his full lips. He had a very fine nose, too. Indeed, he looked like one of the carvings of an angel in the chapel.

That was ridiculous. If this youth were an angel, he was a fallen one, full of sin.

She looked away from his face. His bare arms were all

muscle, without a single bit of fat, like the rest of his body.

She thought of the way he had defended himself. Thin he might be, but he was lean and strong—graceful, almost. And he was certainly an excellent fighter. He could probably hire himself out as a soldier. Noblemen were always seeking men for their garrisons.

Why, if the peasants of Haverleigh could be taught to fight like him, they wouldn't need hired soldiers to protect the estate.

Her breath caught in her throat.

And then she smiled.

CHAPTER TWO

Gavin moaned and put his hand to his aching head. It felt like a band of tiny warriors were shoving spears into it from the inside.

Otherwise, he was warm, and lying on something so marvelously soft that it could not be the ground. Clean linens covered him and a woolen blanket lightly scratched his chin.

He warily opened his eyes to see a beamed ceiling overhead. Light came in through narrow windows shuttered by squares of white cloth.

He eased himself up on his elbows and surveyed the chamber. The walls were of gray stone, not the rough mud and dung spread over woven branches as in a cottage. And he was in a bed—a real bed, with a mattress of straw beneath him. A table with a basin and cloth, an old wooden chest that had once been painted red and blue, and a stand holding a metal pan filled with glowing coals for heating the chamber completed the furnishings.

He could believe he had died and gone to heaven, except for his aching head.

Where was he? How had he come here?

The last thing he remembered was the fight with Fulk, and the dog, which probably belonged to a knight or lord or rich merchant out hunting. Then Fulk had hit him and everything had gone dark.

Since he was not in a dungeon or imprisoned in a cell, Fulk and the others must have run away with the spoils and left him unconscious. Perhaps whoever had found him had assumed he was a traveler who'd been set upon and robbed.

Despite his headache, he grinned at the notion of a thief mistaken for a victim of thieves.

Whatever the people who'd brought him here believed, however, he couldn't stay. Fulk might come back looking for him. Fulk might even decide to rob whoever had taken him in and put him in this wonderful bed and—

By the saints!

He threw back the covers and let out a sigh of relief. Somebody had taken off his tunic and boots, but he still had his breeches on. He felt around his waist and found the small, sharp blade of the knife he kept hidden there.

There was no sign of his tunic or boots, or his sword.

Fulk had probably taken his sword; he would never leave something so valuable behind. Maybe he'd had time to take his boots and tunic, too, which wouldn't surprise him. Fulk was a greedy, rotten scoundrel he should have left long ago.

Meanwhile, here he was with only his breeches and a small knife, everything of value he possessed gone. It served him right for lingering with Fulk, he supposed, instead of striking out on his own and leaving the last remnant of his life with his poor mother.

The stone floor was cold against Gavin's bare feet as he got out of the bed, and he shivered. He went to the chest. His tunic wasn't inside it, but to his surprise and delight, a fine heavy silk tunic of dark blue was. He had brushed against such samite garments when he was cutting purses, but had never actually had one in his hands. It would be worth a lot of money, he thought, as he placed it carefully on the bed.

Next he found a white linen shirt, some breeches made of a very finely woven wool, and beneath those, a pair of soft leather boots much better than his own.

It was a complete set of expensive clothes, and they looked to be about his size.

Were they here on purpose? Was he supposed to find them and put them on? God's wounds, this was puzzling and confusing and, in a way, frightening. Nobody had ever been kind to him without expecting something in return. What would people who gave him such fine clothes want?

He should put on the lot and run away. He could sell these clothes for enough money to feed himself for at least a month.

He considered where he would go—not London, that was certain, lest he encounter Fulk and the others. He ran his hand through his thick hair . . . and didn't encounter a single knot.

Somebody had combed his hair.

This was too strange. He definitely had to get away from here, and as quickly as possible.

With swift movements he drew on the shirt and the boots and then, almost reverently, the tunic.

Now to figure out where exactly he was. He went to the window and looked out—and gripped the sill with all his might as dizziness swamped him.

He was high in a tower of a castle, and the cobblestones of the courtyard below seemed leagues away.

He leaned back against the wall, taking deep breaths. When his heartbeat slowed to near normal, he ventured to look again. Soldiers, horses, and people moved about like so many busy ants.

The courtyard was enclosed by a huge square wall made of gray stone, with wall walks around the top where sentries would patrol. A round tower was at each corner; he was in one of them. Other buildings lined the inner courtyard. It was as if a small village was inside the castle, and another outside.

But what castle was this? Where *was* he?

He wracked his brain for anything that Fulk had said about where they were going. Nothing came to him. All he could remember was that Fulk had thought they should get away from Salisbury after all their thieving there.

He wished he could go out the window, but it was too far to the ground and he would be too visible. He would have to go out the door. Thank God his mother had taught him how to speak well enough to pass for a merchant's son, or even a squire, if he had to. He could surely talk his way out of here. He had talked himself out of tricky predicaments before. As for the clothes, they must expect him to put them on, or they wouldn't have left them there.

He would say he'd been traveling to Salisbury on business for his master—a mason, perhaps—and had been attacked by thieves. He would thank his benefactors for their kindness and the clothes, and walk out the gate.

Perhaps he could slip out into the crowd and through the gate without saying anything to anybody. He had done that sort of thing a hundred times in various towns.

Pleased with his plan, he went to the door, put his hand on the latch, and pushed down.

Nothing happened.

He tried again to be sure.

The door was locked. He was imprisoned in this

room as surely as if he were in the dampest, dankest cell this castle possessed.

He fought the panic and confusion rising within him. Why would somebody save him and then imprison him? Why put him in such a bed and even comb his hair, and then lock him inside?

Because they didn't know anything about him and were wisely being cautious?

He grew a little calmer. Yes, that had to be it.

He pulled out his small knife and slid the blade into the keyhole. A slight twist, and the lock opened. He returned the knife to its place and, keeping his back to the wall, crept slowly down the curving stairs, passing a closed door on another landing. At the bottom, he peered around the final curve into what had to be the great hall of the castle, a vast stone room that made him feel very small and insignificant.

Two people talked together on a dais at the end of the hall near him. Dismissing the well-dressed girl with her back to him, Gavin studied the man dressed in a long black tunic heavily embroidered with gold and silver. He had an expensive scabbard hanging from a thick belt embossed with silver. A red jewel gleamed in the hilt of his sword. About twenty-five, he was tall and well made, with a hawklike nose, and it was obvious he was used to being regarded with respect. He didn't look easy to trick, and suddenly Gavin's strategy seemed doomed to fail.

Sweat trickling down his back, he quickly scanned the rest of the great hall as he tried to come up with an alternate plan. Smoke from the fire in the large round hearth at the center of the chamber curled up toward the high beamed ceiling. The walls were covered with plaster and he could see the hooks where tapestries should be hung, although there were none there now. Around the walls were benches and trestle tables. Their large wooden tops leaned against the walls, with the legs and supports beside them. They could be quickly assembled for meals, and then taken down. The floor of the hall was covered in rushes sprinkled with sweet-smelling herbs like rosemary to ward off the odors of dropped food.

Everything spoke of wealth, comfort, and power.

"I do regret that the earl is unable to see you, my lord," the girl said, drawing his attention. Her voice was refined and musical, yet firmer than he'd expect from a mere girl. "If you had sent a messenger first to inquire, Baron, you would have saved yourself the journey."

Gavin sighed with relief. The man was not the lord, but a guest here. Who, then, was the girl?

He took a better look at her. She wore a plain garment of bright green wool with no decoration. An embroidered belt sat upon her slender hips and a ring of keys hung from it. That and her proud posture told him she must be of high rank here—the lady of the manor, perhaps.

No, she must be the lord's daughter, because she wore nothing over her waving unbound chestnut hair. Married women covered their hair.

She turned slightly, and now he could see that she was very pretty, too, with smooth skin and delicate features.

Envy and bitterness stabbed him. At one time his mother's rank might have made him worthy of such a girl's notice. But his mother's lover had abandoned her, leaving him to a far different fate. He would be lower than a peasant to this youthful lady.

The man smiled, or at least moved his lips in something that was supposed to be a smile. His eyes, though—they gleamed with anger and something else . . . something unsavory and cruel. "I would have sent a messenger had it been only your father I wanted to see, Lady Gwyneth."

"You flatter me, my lord."

Surprisingly, she didn't seem to find the man intimidating at all, in spite of the look in his eyes. Either she was very bold, or very stupid.

"It is the truth," he said.

She gave him another smile, one that did not reach her eyes.

Despite his desire to be gone from here, Gavin couldn't help being impressed. She most certainly was not stupid.

"Perhaps it is well you have come, my lord. I have heard there may be men outside the law on our land. Three rough-looking fellows were recently seen in the wood that borders both our estates."

Gavin shrank back against the wall as if she had turned to point at him.

Then he realized she had said "three." They must think he was indeed a victim and not one of the thieves—but then, why the locked door?

"You have but to ask, and I will send my soldiers to guard Haverleigh," the rich nobleman offered.

Haverleigh. The name meant nothing to Gavin, except that it would be better if he left it as soon as he possibly could.

"I do not think that necessary yet, my lord. It was only three men, and we have nothing here to tempt them."

"There is one thing here that is very tempting."

Gavin peered around the wall again, for he knew that tone. It was how Fulk spoke to a tavern wench.

The girl's lips tightened ever so slightly. Obviously she was not going to be won over by that sort of flattery. "I would ask that you watch out for those men as you return home."

"I shall, and if I find them, they will be duly questioned."

"Will you stay and dine with us?" the girl asked.

"And your escort, too, of course."

The man made a slight bow. "We would be honored, Lady Gwyneth."

"Please excuse me then, Baron DeVilliers, while I inform the cook."

The girl left the man without waiting for him to reply. Fortunately, she didn't even glance at the stairwell as she hurried past.

Meanwhile, the nobleman sat in a tall, high-backed chair and surveyed the room with a pleased smile.

Gavin knew there was no way under heaven he was going to be able to sneak past that smug and watchful visitor. He would have to go back to the chamber and wait until nightfall, when those in the castle would be asleep, except for a few guards on the wall.

Then he recalled that there had been no guards or sentries on the wall walk or anywhere else. All the soldiers he had seen had been on the ground, and idle. They must be this nobleman's guard.

That was strange, too, but the nobleman's offer of soldiers suddenly made more sense.

Yet the girl had refused. Why? Because she preferred to have a vulnerable fortress than be indebted to this man?

He could see why she might not want that . . . but her situation was none of his concern. All he should be thinking about was getting away from here.

If someone came to the room, he decided, he would pretend to be asleep. Then, come night, he would take his leave of this place.

CHAPTER THREE

Balancing a tray covered with a square of linen against her hip, Gwyneth carefully slipped the key in the lock of the upper chamber door. Then she cautiously opened it and peered inside.

The young man was still in bed asleep, his eyes closed. He was still half naked, too.

In the woods she had decided that if Thomas and everyone else at Haverleigh were to believe this young man was a thief's prey and not the thief, she had to make it look as if he'd been robbed before she went for help. Real thieves probably would have stripped him naked, but she hadn't been able to bring herself to do that. Instead, she had hidden his boots and his tunic, and left Rufus standing guard while she hurried to fetch Thomas. His stepson and her friend Hollis had helped, too.

Nobody had spoken to her father or DeVilliers of the stranger from the wood. She had bidden all the servants in the castle to keep quiet about the wounded squire, and she had sent Thomas and Hollis home.

If her plan was to work, people must think this thief was a wounded squire set upon by thieves, stripped of his fine garments, and left for dead. Thanks to his unfortunate mother, the young man sounded as if his status was far above that of a peasant or an outlaw, and she had seen enough of his normal bearing to know he held himself as upright and proudly as any nobleman, despite the circumstances of his birth and life. He could surely pass himself off as a squire—and that was the key to her plan.

She closed the door softly. She set the tray on her brother's old chest and lifted the linen, revealing a small loaf of freshly baked bread, a cup of wine, and four lengths of rope.

She had to make sure that this Gavin could not leave until she had a chance to speak with him and enlist his aid. She took the rope and went to tie his right hand to the side of the bed. His hands were beneath the blanket, so she leaned forward to lift it—and suddenly found herself staring into very wide-awake brown eyes. His left hand shot out from beneath the blanket and grabbed her wrist in a grip of iron.

She frantically tried to pull her hand away. "Let me go or I'll scream!" she cried.

He sat up slowly, studying her intently.

"Who are you? Where am I?" he demanded as he freed her hand. "Why are you tying me to the bed? Are you in league with those thieves who attacked me?"

Stepping away from the bed and rubbing her wrist, she

marveled at the questioning lie that came so easily to his lips. He sounded as haughtily irate as the Baron DeVilliers could, his accent more polished than it had been in the wood. Apparently he was going to play the victim, cleverly assuming the one role that would explain his unconscious presence there.

He would have to be a clever liar if her plan was to succeed, but she would probably never be able to believe a thing he said.

"I am not in league with any thieves," she replied. Inwardly, she added, "Yet."

"Then why were you going to tie me to the bed?"

"For my protection, of course."

"I assure you, kind lady, that I am no danger to you," he said, his low voice as soothing as a cat's purr. "Now, who are you?" He smiled. If she hadn't actually seen him with those other thieves, that smile would have convinced her he was as innocent as a newborn babe. In fact, she could almost believe that now.

She moved back farther still as he swung his long, lean legs out of the bed and put his feet on the floor.

"Gwyneth—*Lady* Gwyneth," she replied hastily. "My father is Lord William, the earl of Haverleigh, and this is his castle."

"Forgive my rude questions, my lady, but naturally I wouldn't expect a noblewoman to tend to a guest, or tie one up, either," he finished with another charming smile.

She could scarcely think with him sitting half naked on the bed, looking at her with that unsettling combination of humility and saucy self-confidence. Although she knew he was a thieving rogue, he looked like a prince with his face clean and his hair combed. He acted like one, too. "I thought it necessary, for my own protection."

"Of course," he answered amicably. "You do not know who I am. My clothes were stolen, I suppose?"

"They were taken, yes."

She went to the wooden chest and threw open the lid. She took out poor Rylan's shirt and tossed it at the handsome young thief, who caught it deftly. The boots, too. She would have given him the tunic, but she might have to sell that soon. "These are my brother's clothes. You may have them."

"That is very generous of you, my lady. Still, I don't think your brother will be pleased to hear you've been giving away his things. Maybe I should leave as I arrived. Or was I completely naked?"

God's wounds, what a thing to say! Her whole body flushed at his bold remark, and even more to see his wry little smile.

"They are yours to keep, and Rylan will not mind," she snapped. "He is dead."

Her blunt words startled the thief, and he dressed without saying anything more, which was as much of a relief as seeing him fully clothed.

"How did I get here, my lady?" he inquired.

"My dog found you."

His eyes narrowed. "A big brute, is he?"

Maybe she should have left Rufus out of it. Well, she had mentioned him, so she had best tell the truth. "Yes."

Gavin sat on the bed and picked up a boot. "How did I get from the wood to your castle?"

"After I found you, I dragged you off the path and covered you with dead leaves and branches until I could fetch help. I went to the reeve, and he and his stepson brought you here."

The thief paused in the act of pulling on the second boot. "You were in the wood alone?"

Perhaps her unprotected ramble was something she should keep secret. She strolled toward the window, then turned to face him. "I was with my maidservants."

She could see doubt in his eyes. The impudent rascal. Nobody had ever doubted her word before. Of course, she had never had cause to be so bluntly dishonest before, either. "What is your name?"

He got to his feet. "Gavin, my lady."

That, at least, was the truth. "Where are you from, Gavin?"

He sauntered toward her. "Nottingham."

That was a lie, for it wouldn't explain his accent in the wood, which was indiscernible now. He sounded as if he came directly from the king's court.

He came closer, reminding her of one of the barn cats stalking an unsuspecting mouse. Should she move away, or stand her ground? She had no idea as he closed the space between them.

"I thank you for your generous hospitality, my lady," he said in a low tone that seemed to make something inside her quiver, "but I really must be on my way. I have urgent business to attend to for my master."

She planted her feet and crossed her arms, determined to act upon her plan. "You have to stay."

He frowned, his dark brows lowering. "*Have* to? Nay, I dare not. If I feel well enough to travel, I must, or my master will be angry."

"No, he won't. You have no master."

Gavin's frown deepened. "Why do you think that?"

"Because I saw you in the wood *before* you were hurt."

His expression grew stern as he grabbed her shoulders and pulled her close. His lips curled into a sardonic smile and his brown eyes seemed to flash with scorn. "A fine game you've been playing, with me the dupe. What will you do, lady? Turn me over to the king's justice? If you think to do that, you had better have more than ropes here."

She reached into her belt and pulled out her brother's dagger which she had hidden there, putting the tip of the blade against his throat. "As you see, I do. Let me go."

Still glaring at her, he did. "If you know what I am, why am I not imprisoned, or turned over to that nobleman?"

"What nobleman?"

Gavin's expression altered, as if he was annoyed with himself—another little shadow of weakness in him that strengthened her. "The man in the black robe I saw in the courtyard."

"I wouldn't hand over a thief discovered on our estate to a visiting nobleman. My father rules Haverleigh in the king's name. He has the right to judge you in the king's name."

The thief's gaze didn't waver. "Then why didn't you bring me before him?"

"My father is ill at the moment. The running of the estate is in my hands."

"You look young for such responsibility."

Gwyneth's blue eyes turned to ice and her grip on the dagger tightened. "I am old enough. I have a use for you."

"Indeed?" he asked, one brow quirked in query as he eyed the dagger in her hands. "So that is why you put me here in this room and that fine bed. What is this use you have for me that requires you to house a thief in a fine chamber and give him such expensive clothes? You've treated me like a guest, except for the locked door. And the dagger at my throat, of course."

Before she could answer, a look of sudden comprehension dawned in his brown eyes.

"Somebody undressed me and combed my hair," he murmured as he circled her. "And I would have to be a fool not to know girls find me handsome. Since I am not a fool, I believe you do, too. Is that why you took pity on me, my young and pretty lady? Is that why you combed my hair and gave me your brother's clothes? What use have you for me here?"

She blushed hotly as she answered him. "You are an insolent rascal!"

"Sometimes." He smiled as he halted in front of her. "Don't you like rascals, my lady? Don't you find us exciting?"

"No! Thief or not, I couldn't leave you there in the woods. You might have died from the cold."

His gaze seemed to bore into her, as if he would seek the answers to his questions that way. "Why not let me die? I am nothing except a thief and a cutpurse, fit only for hanging."

She grew warm under his steadfast gaze, but she would not—could not—let him discomfit her.

"What other use could you have for me, my lady, save as some kind of pet?" His gaze hardened, reminding her of the life he had led, and that he was not a chivalrous nobleman. "If that is what you want of me, you had better think again, because as difficult as it may be for a woman of your class to understand, I have my pride, too. Now I want to leave, and although I don't want to hurt you, I will if you try to stop me." He strode toward the door.

"As you say, you are a good fighter," she declared. "I

want you to teach our tenants to be good fighters, too."

Gavin halted abruptly and slowly wheeled to face her. He couldn't have been more surprised if she had asked him to rule England.

"You want me to teach your tenants how to fight?" he repeated incredulously.

"How to fight *well*," she clarified, as if that was the most important thing of all.

Her proposition was, quite simply, unbelievable, and his mind cried caution. "Where is the castle garrison?"

Although Lady Gwyneth still faced him defiantly, a pink flush stole up her cheeks, hinting that perhaps she was not quite so brave and bold as she seemed. "They left when we could no longer afford to pay them."

"Didn't they swear an oath of loyalty to your father?"

"They were hired foot soldiers. Our estate is too small to provide for knights as well."

He gestured at the walls, the furnishings. "Aren't you rich?"

"Compared to you, I suppose we are, yet we cannot afford to keep a garrison anymore. But there are enough tenants to protect the castle and their farms on our land, if need be. Unfortunately, they don't know how to wield swords. You do, and I would have them learn."

It still sounded too simple, too easy, and utterly unbelievable. "Protect them from who?"

She blushed again, more deeply this time, from her slender throat to the roots of her bountiful brown hair. "From greedy men who think they can take Haverleigh from my father and me."

Like the man he had seen below on the dais. From the way he had looked at this pretty girl, he wanted more than her home. That might explain why she sounded desperate.

Yet why should he pity her or have any concern for her fate? Gavin asked himself. She was far better off than he had ever been, as her fine gown of soft green wool showed. If she had to marry a man she didn't like, it would not be unusual for one of her class. Marriages were arranged for political and financial reasons all the time among the nobility. At least she would not be thrown out into the world with no way to earn her keep.

"My people do not know you are a peasant and a thief," she continued, finally putting the dagger back into the belt at her narrow waist. "I'm going to tell them you are a knight's squire who was traveling to Salisbury from the north. I will explain that you have offered to instruct them to show your thanks for our help."

She clasped her hands together and gazed at him with a steadiness he found disturbing. It was as if she were trying to see into his heart. "If you are a squire, they must accord you respect because of your rank, and while you are here, you will have all the rights and privileges such rank accords you."

The rights and privileges of a squire. Respect. Good food. Clean clothes, and a bed to sleep in every night. Servants to wait upon him.

The life he might have had, had his mother married his father. He did not know whether the man who had sired him had been noble or not. Indeed, he might have been a groom, for all Gavin knew, but he'd always imagined that his father had been a knight, albeit a less than chivalrous one, to abandon his mother the way he had.

And he would have this pretty young lady's company, too.

Her offer was very tempting, if he could trick her tenants into believing he was a squire for a little while.

That was the fly in the oil.

"You believe I could pass for a knight's squire?" he demanded.

"In the woods you sounded a bit like a Scot. It is well known that the Scots are almost barbarians. They will excuse anything odd you do because of that."

He leaned his weight on one leg and crossed his arms as he regarded her. "You've thought this all out, haven't you?"

She nodded.

"And you expect your people to believe this incredible story?"

She drew herself up, the very picture of a proud young

noblewoman. "They will because *I* tell it."

He wasn't nearly as convinced that her word alone would make her plan work.

But who am I to refuse a lady? he thought with grim sarcasm. He might as well stay, at least for the time being, unless her plan proved faulty from the start. He would have more comfortable lodgings than any he had ever had before, and while he trained her men, he would enjoy a squire's privileges.

Indeed, the more he contemplated Lady Gwyneth's surprising offer, the more he liked it—provided he was not in danger. The moment this plan seemed about to fail, though, he would flee. "For how long would I have to stay here and teach them?"

"Until I think they are ready. I have seen my father's soldiers drill many times, so I will know. We won't start today, however, because we have a guest. Tomorrow he'll be gone, and you can begin then."

Gavin smiled his most charming smile and gave her what he thought was a very excellent bow. "I am pleased to be of service, my lady."

"You bowed too quickly. A nobleman would take more time, and raise his eyes at the end to look at me, to make sure I was looking at him. Do it again."

"I thought *I* was to be the teacher," he remarked as he obeyed.

"Of fighting, yes. If you are to pass as a squire, you

will have to learn a few manners, too." Then she gave him a smile, and a strange, unfamiliar warmth blossomed within him.

The last time anybody had looked on him with approval was when he had stolen a lord's purse full of silver coins. Then Fulk had gone out and gotten drunk with most of it. Her approval was far more pleasant.

"I've brought you some food." As she gestured at the tray, he realized how hungry he was. "Eat now."

"Thank you, my lady," he said. He reached out and caressed her soft cheek. "It smells nearly as good as you."

Her expression altered, and he found himself looking into eyes that shone with a fierceness he had never seen in a girl's eyes before. "Don't bother with any attempts to charm me, Gavin. Don't forget I know who and what you really are. And do not think of running away before the men are ready. If you do, I will raise a hue and cry, and every man and boy in Haverleigh will search for you. You wouldn't be able to get very far."

"And if they catch me?" he asked with another smile, ignoring what she'd said about using his charm. She could protest all she wanted, but he had seen the way she'd looked at him. She wasn't immune to him.

"You will be hanged."

Without another word, Lady Gwyneth marched out of the chamber, slamming the door behind her.

He stared after her. By the saints, she sounded absolutely heartless. Maybe he was a fool to think she saw him as anything but a thief who could train her peasants. To believe otherwise might be a terrible mistake.

Then he realized he had not heard the key turn in the lock.

CHAPTER FOUR

Much later, when all sounds of life in the castle had died away and no one was in the courtyard, Gavin cautiously opened the chamber door.

Time to show Lady Gwyneth what he thought of her haughty manner and ultimatums.

And why not go? He didn't owe her anything. Surely he would have survived one night in the wood. He might have been thirsty and stiff when he awakened, but nothing more—unless Fulk had come back to finish him off, to ensure that he couldn't tell anyone about his former comrades.

No, Fulk and the others were probably far away.

Besides, the girl's scheme was ridiculous. After thinking more about it, and after the initial thrill of playing a role previously denied him had passed, he had realized he could probably never trick anyone into believing he was a squire for long, no matter where she said he was from. Her people would guess he was an impostor, she would decide it was wiser to claim he had tricked her, and he would be thrown in the dungeon and convicted for thieving. Then he would be hanged. Only a fool would trust that she could keep him safe, even if she wanted to.

Firm in his resolve, Gavin crept out of the chamber and began to make his way down the steps.

As he drew near the other room that opened from the circular stairway, he heard soft voices. A beam of feeble light shone through the open door. As he cautiously approached, he paused a moment to see who was in the room.

Lady Gwyneth sat on a low stool beside a very tall, very ornate bed, the posts carved with leaves and vines. It had thick curtains of dark red cloth that were opened enough for him to see a thin, white-haired man lying there.

The few other furnishings were far plainer than the bed, as if the owner was not rich anymore, yet kept a few items from the days when he had been. The light came from a small oil lamp set upon the table beside the bed, its golden glow illuminating the profile of Lady Gwyneth.

"You will soon be better, Father," she murmured as she stroked the old man's hand.

"I hope so, daughter," the earl rasped, his breathing labored. "Was that the baron I heard bellowing in the courtyard?"

Lady Gwyneth smiled. "Yes. He has stayed the night, but he leaves in the morning."

"Good. The man is like a carrion crow, always in

black." Lord William started to cough, making his whole body shake in a way that made Gavin frown. The man sounded very far from well.

"And the garrison commander?" the earl continued after Lady Gwyneth had helped him take a drink from the goblet by his bed. "Not giving you any trouble, I hope?"

"No, he obeys me. He doesn't like the passwords I assign, but I have run out of names of weapons and great generals."

Gavin's brow furrowed with puzzlement. She had said before that they had no soldiers, and he had seen none upon the wall walk or at sentry positions. She must be lying to her father.

God's wounds, she was a bold creature . . . or desperate not to worry him.

Gavin leaned closer, wondering if she was going to tell the earl about him, and whether it would be the truth, or the tale she had concocted.

"And Thomas?" the earl asked.

"He also obeys."

Her father sighed wearily and shook his head. "Ah, but reluctantly, I'm sure. Thomas thinks all females have no sense, and young ones most of all."

"You are not to worry about anything, Father. All is well in hand. Sleep now. You need your rest."

Gavin drew back. All was well in hand? With a girl in

charge of a castle, and a man like that carrion crow—
a most apt description!—hovering about, ready to take
this castle from the earl and make his daughter his wife?

What did their troubles have to do with him? Lady
Gwyneth had threatened him with hanging. It was time
to go.

"I know what he wants, you know," the old man said.

Gavin's curiosity rooted him to the step and he peered
through the door again.

"You must not agree, Gwyneth. He is not the man for
you. You deserve someone better."

"I assure you, Father, I have no plan to accept the
baron as my husband. I have another . . ." She fell silent as
she got to her feet.

"Another?" the earl wheezed.

"Another task I must complete before I retire." She
patted his hand. "Now we have talked long enough. Semeli
will be wondering where I am."

The old man nodded, and his eyes closed. "Good
night, my daughter. I rest easy, knowing you are in charge."

As Gwyneth started for the door, Gavin darted back
up the stairs toward his chamber.

Then he realized she was coming up the stairs after
him. Foolish, unreasonable panic seized him and he ran
into the room.

As he listened, his ear to the closed door, he heard her
steps come to a stop outside. She waited a moment, as if

she were listening, too, and he wondered if she could hear him panting.

He waited anxiously for her to open the door and demand to know what he was doing, or at least check to see if he was there. She didn't.

Instead, he heard the key turn, locking the door. Then her footsteps slowly died away.

"Has my father eaten anything yet?" Gwyneth asked her maidservant as Semeli braided her hair the next morning.

Mercifully, DeVilliers and his band of men had ridden out at first light, before she could have been expected to bid him farewell. She suspected it was really the better food waiting for him at home that sent him rushing away, but she didn't really care.

She glanced at her friend in her mirror and wished she dared tell Semeli the truth about Gavin. Gwyneth had never kept a secret from her before, not from the time Semeli and her mother had joined the household of Haverleigh when both girls were four years old.

Semeli and her exotic mother had been slaves, owned by a Norse trader who had presented them to the earl as a gift, no doubt in hopes of future dealings. The earl had accepted the gift, then told the Norseman he would not bargain with such a man, *ever*. Slavery was something he had never condoned, although it was certainly no crime.

He had freed Semeli and her mother at once. Semeli's mother had become Gwyneth's mother's maidservant, and it seemed only natural that Semeli and Gwyneth have the same relationship. These days Semeli insisted on performing a maidservant's duties, and since it was a matter of some pride to her, Gwyneth agreed. That also meant they could be together much of the time, and they were far more friends than mistress and maid.

"This morning your father ate a little more than yesterday. I am sure he is growing stronger," Semeli said, her accent carrying a hint of the far-off land where her mother had been born.

Semeli herself had never been there, but with her dark, exotic looks and accent, and the swaying, graceful way she moved, it was clear to all who saw her that she was not Saxon, Norman, Norse, or Celt, despite the clothes she wore.

"I hope you're right," Gwyneth answered. "And surely the next harvest will be a better one. Then we'll be able to hire soldiers again."

She eyed Semeli in her mirror. "The injured squire I found in the wood yesterday has made a very interesting proposition," she said, sounding as matter-of-fact as she could. "He noticed there were no sentries and was most chivalrously concerned for our safety here. I explained about my father's illness and our . . . lack of funds. Then he said he was in no hurry to get to Salisbury, so in thanks for my rescue, he'll gladly stay here a little while and train the men of Haverleigh to be soldiers."

Gwyneth had never seen Semeli look so stunned. "Teach our men to be soldiers?" she echoed incredulously.

Gwyneth twisted on her stool to face her. "Yes, or at least able to defend the castle. There is room here for all the village to take sanctuary, if necessary. If our men can offer some defense, the baron will have to think twice about trying to take Haverleigh by force."

Semeli's eyes widened. "It is no secret that the baron covets Haverleigh, but do you think he would really try to take it by force? Your father is the rightful lord."

"If the baron thought he could get away with it, and if I refuse to marry him, *and* if my father is slow to recover, I would not put it past him. If I accept Gavin's offer, DeVilliers will discover he won't be able to simply ride up to the gates one day and take it."

Semeli still looked skeptical, and Gwyneth began to despair that her plan was ridiculous, for if Semeli did not believe in it, how would the men of Haverleigh respond? "I think Gavin can do it. He seems very competent."

"How would you know that?"

That was, unfortunately, a very good question, but she could not tell Semeli of the fight she had witnessed in the wood. "He told me, and I believe him. Besides, one has only to look at his muscles to see that he must be quite . . . quite . . ."

"Quite?" Semeli prompted, a sparkle of amusement replacing her doubt.

"Quite a fighter."

"I would have looked, had you not sent me to sit with your father."

"Yes, well, Gavin was in no state to have many visitors. He wasn't seriously injured, but he did need to rest."

"I understand. And you noticed his muscles while he slept."

Gwyneth silently cursed the blush she could feel spreading upon her face. "What of it if I did?"

"He seems to have made quite an impression on you, that's all. And you are sure he can teach our men?"

"He says he can, and I think I would be foolish not to accept this opportunity. Every day we can keep the baron at bay is another day for my father to recover, so that he can rule Haverleigh again. Until then, we are vulnerable."

"Yes, I see the merit in your plan," Semeli gravely agreed. "Besides, it is better to take action than sit and worry." Then her smile blossomed. "If this Gavin is also a handsome young man . . . well . . . that cannot be helped."

Gwyneth gave her friend a sour look. "I don't care *what* he looks like as long as our men learn what he can teach them. Now, if you will excuse me, I had better go rouse our guest to go to mass. Who is with my father?"

"Peg."

"She'll be more asleep than awake," Gwyneth said, her pique fading as she thought of her kindhearted old nurse, "but with luck he will sleep, too. I'm sure if he wakes and needs anything, she'll be able to fetch someone to help."

"I shall look in on them both," Semeli assured her, thankfully without further mention of Gavin or his appearance.

"I'll need to summon one man from every household," Gwyneth said. "Will you take the message to Thomas?"

Although there was no love lost between Semeli and the village reeve, Gwyneth knew Semeli would welcome any chance to speak to Thomas's stepson.

"If Thomas gives you any trouble about it, tell him it is my father's order that his tenants come as part of their obligation to their overlord."

It was another lie, but she didn't mind lying to Thomas any more than she'd have minded lying to the baron.

"I'll need them only half a day," she continued. "That shouldn't interfere with the work on the farms or at their trade too much." She chewed her lip. "I'd reduce the tithes if I could, too, but then I wouldn't be able to pay the taxes at all."

Semeli nodded and patted her arm. "I'm sure they will come. They do not want to see a new lord at Haverleigh, either."

After leaving her chamber, which was in the tower

opposite her father's and Gavin's, Gwyneth hurried down the worn steps.

She nearly collided with Thomas, who was waiting at the bottom of the stairs.

The stocky reeve looked as startled as she felt. Recovering from the shock, he ran a wide hand over his balding head and straightened his tunic. Like most men of his rank, he was dressed in a brown woolen tunic, breeches, and boots. His were a bit finer than some, for he was a well-to-do merchant, which was one reason he had been chosen for this position, the liaison between the earl and his villagers. He could spare the time from his business without financial loss, and he had a knack for figures. Nobody could keep a tally in his head like Thomas.

As for his features, Thomas's expression had settled into a frown years ago, resulting in perpetual furrows in his brow and cheeks.

"I'm sorry," Gwyneth said, steadying herself. "I wasn't expecting to see you in the hall so early, Thomas. I hope it isn't trouble that brings you here at this time of day."

"My lady, as you know, I take my duties as reeve of Haverleigh very seriously."

Gwyneth pressed her lips together to subdue a sigh and keep herself from scowling. This was the way Thomas began every complaint against every decision she made, and as always when he spoke to her, Thomas's tone had an undercurrent of disapproval, as if having to report to a fifteen-year-old girl was a personal insult to him. However, while her father was sick, Haverleigh was in her care and Thomas would simply have to accept it.

"I must ask you to reconsider the baron's offer of troops for protection," he continued. "Without a garrison, our village and this castle are all too open to attack."

She was not surprised Thomas had heard of the baron's offer, nor was she surprised he wanted her to accept it. The baron, after all, was a man. Better a cruel, greedy master than the earl's young daughter in charge, he obviously believed.

Gwyneth straightened her shoulders. "My father and I have decided to train one man from every household to fight like a soldier to defend his home and Haverleigh. That young man we rescued in the forest yesterday is a squire, and he is going to teach them, as his thanks for our help."

Thomas's mouth gaped and his frown deepened even more. "That's absurd!"

She raised her brow as her father did when he wanted to remind somebody that they were addressing the earl of Haverleigh. "I do not recall my father asking your opinion, Thomas." With inward satisfaction, she saw the tips of Thomas's ears redden. "Now, if you will excuse me, I must see if our guest is awake."

"But, my lady—"

Once again she regarded Thomas with all the proud majesty she could muster. "As I said before, my father has agreed. Or do you no longer wish to be reeve?"

"No, my lady," Thomas replied, his gaze finally faltering. "It shall be as your father orders."

Breathing a small sigh of relief, Gwyneth left him and hurried toward the north tower, pausing in the doorway of her father's chamber. Peg smiled and waved gaily from her place beside the earl's bed. He was sleeping peacefully these days, not tossing and turning as he had during the worst of the fever.

Gwyneth continued on her way, and once outside the upper chamber, took a moment to draw in a deep breath and remember that she was Lady Gwyneth of Haverleigh. The young man awaiting her was not a lord, or a knight, or even a squire. While he was very handsome, that should not influence or intimidate her one whit.

Her resolve was tested the instant she stepped inside the chamber and Gavin turned toward her, away from the window.

Dressed in Rylan's clothes, standing there as proud as anybody, he appeared to be every inch a squire. Indeed, with his broad shoulders and handsome face, he looked more like a young nobleman than many a squire she had met.

Despite her best efforts, the warm heat of a blush crept up her face as he ran his gaze over her, while her pride commanded that she not look away.

He grinned suddenly, a roguish grin such as no squire had ever given her before. The unexpectedness of it was like the sun appearing on a cloudy day.

"How do I look?" he asked. "Presentable?"

"You look well enough," she said shortly, trying not to notice just how good he did look. She gestured at the window. "It's a long way down. I think you would break your neck if you tried to get out that way."

"I saw your guest leave. Early for him to go, wasn't it? Did you send him away on my account?"

"No, although it is much better he never saw you. I fear he finds our plain fare not to his liking."

"Ah." Gavin crossed his arms and leaned back against the sill, as casually as if he had lived there all his life. "There is quite a crowd gathering in the courtyard," he noted.

"One man from every household is coming because the lady of Haverleigh summons them," she announced in as cold and haughty a tone as she could manage. "They are the men you must convince that you are a squire, and if you have had a change of heart or think to run away, remember what I said about a hue and cry."

Gavin straightened, and the intense, arrogant look that came to his dark brown eyes suddenly made it seem that he loomed closer, although his feet did not move. "I know what I am, too, my lady, and I know what you can do to me, if you choose, whether I train your men or not."

Her threat could not be helped. She must be in control here. He had to do what she said, even if he had a way of making her feel weak and strong at the same time, as if part of her wanted to tell him all her troubles though her pride argued against it. "If you teach them, when they are ready, you will be completely free to go."

He walked toward her. "Really?"

"You have the word of Lady Gwyneth of Haverleigh."

He ran a long, slow, measuring gaze over her, starting at her toes and traveling up her entire body. It was all she could do not to squirm, or turn away, or shout at him to stop.

"Since I have no choice," he said, "I must accept the word of Lady Gwyneth of Haverleigh and hope she keeps it."

"Of course I will. Now, come. The men should all be here now. We will attend mass, and then—" He had not moved, and his full lips had twisted with a scowl. "What is it?"

"I've never been to mass, and I have no intention of going today, either," he said, his voice as hard as the stones in the wall behind him.

She couldn't believe it. "You've *never* been to mass?"

He shook his head. "No."

"But your soul—"

"Is doomed already. I've never been baptized, either."

She had to sit down on the bed. "I've never met

anyone who wasn't a Christian."

"If you were damned from the womb and your mother denied Christian burial, you might not attend church, either."

"The child is not responsible for his mother's sins," she protested, "and the Church dispenses charity."

His eyes flared with a deep bitterness that seemed to make a mockery of all she knew. "My lady, you have not lived much among the world, have you? If so, you would know that not every man who lives in Holy Orders is good, or even what you would call a Christian."

Annoyed by his superior tone, she pushed away her sympathy for both the boy he had been and his mother, and spoke with grim determination. "While I regret your experience of the Church has apparently not been pleasant, the fact remains that if you are to be believed to be a squire, you must attend mass. Otherwise, I will have no choice but to imprison you."

"A forced conversion, then, my lady?" he asked mockingly as he strolled closer.

"If that is what you want to call it, yes," she replied, wishing he had stayed by the window. It was easier to think when he was farther away. "But do not take the holy wafer. That would be too sinful. We shall say . . ." She paused a moment and tapped her lip with her fingertip as she considered. "We shall say you are waiting until you make your confession in the cathedral at Salisbury."

He circled her, and she had the uncomfortable feeling that he was like a hawk searching for a mouse in the field below. "Your priest will accept that?"

"Father Bernard is a good man who has known me since birth. He will not question me."

Gavin's voice came from behind her. "Is it not wrong to lie to a man of God?"

Unfortunately, he was right. Shame filled her at the thought of what she was going to have to do. "When you've gone, I'll confess everything."

Gavin halted in front of her, a sardonic expression on his face. "That makes it all right?"

She had enough to worry about without this thief making her feel she was putting her mortal soul in jeopardy, too. Her whole body quivered with righteous indignation as she jabbed his chest with her finger, making him move back. "Listen to me, *thief*. I am fighting for my family's home in the only way I can. I will do what I must, and I hope God will understand. I don't care if *you* do or not, so long as you do what you're told!"

His scowling gaze bored into her and the golden tints in his angry brown eyes flashed like fires of rage.

"Very well, my fine lady," he retorted, moving forward so that she had to back away. "You have me as good as in a noose, after all. I cannot leave, and I am safe only as long as I am in your good graces. You are superior to me in birth and everything else." He bowed, his whole manner insolent. "Forgive me if I forgot that for a brief moment. I will never forget it again. But since you are so superior to me in every way, perhaps *you* should train your men, not me."

Gwyneth stiffened. "If I had been taught to wield a sword myself, I would. My education did not include that."

"How unfortunate for you, then."

"Yes!"

His lips curved into a cold smile that had more of hate in it than merriment. "It must be terrible for you to need someone like me."

She stumbled away from him and his anger, as her own filled her and made her strong. "Yes, it's terrible," she cried, regaining her balance, and her pride. "It's humiliating! I wish my father were well, and my brother alive, so things could be as they were—but they aren't. So I must humble myself to ask for a thief's help. Are you satisfied now, Gavin? Are you pleased to hear how desperate I am?"

The fires in his eyes were banked as quickly as they had arisen. "Yes."

Confused, she could only stare at him as he came toward her. Feeling helpless to stop him, she let him take her hands in his, the warmth and the power of his lean, strong fingers seeming to fly along her limbs toward her very heart. "You can threaten me all you like, my lady, but you need me. Do you agree, or shall we end this now? You can hang me if you must and find somebody else to train your tenants."

She pulled her hands from his grasp, her reluctance to do so startling and unexpected. "Very well," she muttered. "I need you."

"What was that? I couldn't hear you."

She shot him a fierce look. "I need you."

He nodded, just once, and then he smiled.

"*For now*," she sternly clarified. "And do not try to malinger. I shall know if you are delaying on purpose."

His smile faded. "My lady, I have no wish to be your dog longer than I must."

"Good. Now, put out your arm to escort me."

He did, bending his elbow perfectly and holding it away from his body.

Her eyes narrowed.

"I haven't been living in a cave somewhere," he said. "I've seen well-to-do men with their wives and daughters."

Fighting to regain her calm, Gwyneth slipped her arm through his. As their bodies touched, she tried to ignore the unfamiliar heat coursing through her. After all, other men and youths had escorted her. It must be because of their argument that she felt so disconcerted. "We had better hurry, or they will be wondering what keeps us."

She walked forward, but he didn't move. It was as if he yanked her to a halt. "What's the matter now?" she demanded.

He smiled slowly, and the golden glints in his eyes seemed to sparkle with smug satisfaction. "If I am the squire, shouldn't I lead you, my lady, and not the other way around?"

She was not happy to realize he was right.

CHAPTER FIVE

His head bowed, his hands clasped so tightly together that his knuckles were white, Gavin stood beside Lady Gwyneth in the small stone chapel of Haverleigh Castle, silently cursing. He hated being here, and he hated Lady Gwyneth for forcing him to come. Not only did he have no use for a church that had no mercy on his poor mother, he was used to blending in, to becoming part of the crowd, the better to cut purses and slip away unnoticed. To stand here at the front, where everybody could see him . . . it was nearly enough to make him wish Fulk and the others had dragged him off with them.

As for passing himself off as a squire—surely it would take more than fine clothes to fool the priest, if not the rest of these people.

And would a gathering of grown men really believe a girl's lies, even if she was the daughter of their lord?

He glanced up at Father Bernard, who was praying in Latin. The priest wore dark robes, and the top of his gray head was shaved to make a tonsure.

When the incense started wafting through the small building, it was all Gavin could do not to cough. At last the time came for the priest to offer the host, the blessed bread that Gavin shouldn't take for fear of damnation and offending Lady Gwyneth, who ordered him about as if he were Rufus.

Lady Gwyneth approached the altar.

Everyone here would be suspicious if he didn't take the bread, so why not? He wasn't baptized and he was a thief, so he was already damned anyway.

He boldly strode forward to stand beside Lady Gwyneth. Her shoulders tensed as the priest put the holy bread in his mouth.

Despite his defiant resolution, Gavin half expected it to burst into flames on contact with his tongue. When it didn't, he swallowed it quickly and sauntered back to his place. Once there, he bowed his head and assumed a virtuous expression of the sort he had seen on the faces of those who sold expensive holy relics they made themselves out of chicken bones and bits of wood.

After some more praying, he realized the mass must be concluded. *Thank God*, he thought, the words the only sort of prayer he ever said.

Lady Gwyneth put her hand on his arm and squeezed hard enough to hurt. "We can go now," she whispered, her lips barely moving, her blue eyes fairly jumping with rage.

All his life, he had been led to believe that noble ladies

were delicate, almost sickly creatures who would faint at the merest hint of trouble or inconvenience. Either he had been misled, or the people who had spoken thus had never met anybody like Lady Gwyneth.

She really was a very confusing girl, vulnerable one moment, stern and forbidding the next. So pretty and feminine in her looks, yet with a bold spirit that flashed unbidden from her bright blue eyes.

He wasn't sure if that contradiction was a good thing or not.

Trying to act as if her anger didn't bother him a bit and telling himself it really didn't, he held out his arm as he had before. She slipped hers through it, barely touching him.

The circle of various keys tied to the leather belt around her hips bounced and jingled with her brisk pace as she marched beside him, so stiff and formal in her plain dark blue gown, her hair braided so that he could see the slender white nape of her neck. In the courtyard under the slate gray sky, there was a crowd waiting for them. For *him*. The older men, who looked a lot less pleased to be there, stood behind the excited young ones.

The older men had probably seen many noblemen come to the castle and pass through the village. They were the ones he would have to convince—perhaps most especially the bald man with the deep frown who looked as if he would doubt the Archangel Gabriel had he appeared in a blaze of light to announce his divine presence.

Gavin's first instinct was to cut and run, to get away from the danger such scrutiny usually brought. Only the sensation of Lady Gwyneth's arm in his prevented him from doing just that.

"I will introduce you before we break the fast," she said in a whisper. "Head for that tall lad there, in the gray wool tunic."

Gavin grudgingly did as he'd been told. The youth, who seemed to be about Gavin's age, had reddish brown hair that stuck up in several places, a wide mouth that seemed on the verge of breaking into a grin, freckles across an upturned nose, and brown eyes that danced with merriment.

"Gavin of Inverlea, this is Hollis," Lady Gwyneth said, her clipped words telling Gavin that she was still annoyed with him.

Fine. He was annoyed with her, too.

And where the devil was Inverlea? Was it even a real place, or had Lady Gwyneth concocted it out of thin air? What other tales was she going to make up that he might have to remember?

"Good day," Hollis said, bowing low, yet with a saucy air, as if he accorded few men respect simply because of their birth.

"Good day to you," Gavin replied in a broad Scots accent.

Indeed, it was so pronounced that as he looked around and saw everyone's confused expressions, he realized nobody could understand him. He had better not exaggerate it quite so much.

"Hollis is Thomas the reeve's stepson, and this is Thomas," Lady Gwyneth said, introducing him to the frowning bald man who appeared even more disgruntled than before.

As the reeve, Thomas would surely make a fine rent collector, if you wanted someone who looked like he wouldn't mind breaking somebody's head if they couldn't pay, Gavin thought grimly.

"Thomas and his stepson brought you here from the wood," Lady Gwyneth explained.

If he was to do what she wanted, he'd have to convince this skeptical man, so he assumed what he thought an appropriately arrogant manner. "I, Gavin of Inverlea, thank you for your assistance, Thomas."

Thomas continued to regard Gavin with obvious suspicion. "It's lucky for us a fine squire like you happened to be robbed in our wood, and that you've decided to stay to train our men to fight, since the earl can't afford to keep soldiers. I'm surprised you aren't in any hurry to get back to your master."

"I am on a pilgrimage to the cathedral in Salisbury

before I am knighted," Gavin replied with a suitably noble drawl. "The knight I serve is out of the country, so I have his leave to take my time."

"You had no escort, no guard?"

"The men I hired proved themselves cowards the moment those ruffians appeared. My guard fled like frightened children, and I haven't seen them since." He waved his hand in airy dismissal. "Good riddance to them, I must say. I have no desire to have such creatures in my employ."

Thomas's eyes gleamed like a weasel's. "You didn't say what knight you serve. A fine fellow like you, I'm sure he's an important one. Who is it?"

Gavin blurted out the first name that came to his mind. "Sir Henry D'Argent."

Lady Gwyneth's grip tightened on his arm so hard, he could feel her nails digging into his arm. Everybody else in the courtyard gasped, and even Thomas looked surprised. "You serve Henry D'Argent? The man who's won every tournament in England for the past three years?"

By the saints, he'd been a fool! Of the five official tournament fields in England, one was near Salisbury. Some of these men might have gone there and actually seen D'Argent, while Gavin had never laid eyes on the man. He should have made up a name.

Then he told himself it might not be so bad. They might have seen D'Argent, but they would not have noticed his squire.

His confidence somewhat restored, Gavin pulled away from Lady Gwyneth, crossed his arms, and leaned his weight on one leg as he calmly surveyed the reeve. "Yes, I serve *Sir* Henry D'Argent. Tell me, Thomas, do you question all the guests of your overlord and his charming daughter in this blunt fashion, or is it a special honor you have reserved for me?"

Thomas flushed, but he didn't back down. "I am the shire reeve. It's my business to know what's going on in Haverleigh."

"You know what's going on," Lady Gwyneth answered. "This fine young man has volunteered to teach our men to defend our home, and my father has accepted his offer. It is not your place, Thomas, to question my father's decisions, or interrogate our guests."

Thomas scowled, but he nodded and stepped back— because of *her*, not because of the supposed squire addressing him. That observation disgruntled Gavin. Meanwhile, the other men exchanged secretive smiles, as if they were delighted to see Thomas chastised by anybody.

All except the lad Hollis. He was staring at something behind Gwyneth, and a rather stunned smile bloomed upon his face.

Gavin turned to see what he was looking at.

A young woman was approaching. She seemed about the same age as Lady Gwyneth, but in every other way she was very different. She was taller, and her skin was a light brown. She had enormous dark eyes, and her whole body swayed when she walked, as if she had willow branches for bones. Her bearing seemed as regal as a queen's, yet her clothing, while neat and clean, marked her as a servant in the household.

She came to a halt and ran a slow, measuring gaze over him, as if Gavin were a horse for sale at a market.

Surely that was no way for any servant to regard a squire, no matter how she carried herself. Raising a brow, he glanced at Lady Gwyneth. "Who is this?"

"This is Semeli." He thought he saw amusement dancing in Lady Gwyneth's eyes as she answered—hardly the way to treat a respected guest.

In retaliation, he ran an equally measuring gaze over Semeli, in a way that would have made several other girls he had met in his travels blush to the roots of their hair.

Semeli did smile, but it was an indulgent one, as if he were a little child. "I bid you welcome to Haverleigh," she said with a very graceful bow. "I am the servant of Lady Gwyneth."

Intrigued by her accent, he asked, "Are you a Moor?"

She raised her chin with elegant pride. "I am a princess of Persia."

This was so surprising and unexpected, he had to wonder if it could possibly be true. He glanced again at Lady Gwyneth, whose bland expression was utterly and frustratingly unreadable.

So he looked at Hollis, who did not seem to be quite conscious, although his eyes were open. If ever Gavin had seen a man besotted by a woman, he was seeing it now.

"I was born a princess in Persia," Semeli said, "but my mother and I were stolen away by Norse pirates."

Gavin had heard that Norsemen sailed far and wide, and traded in slaves, so her history could very well be true.

"If you require anything to make your stay here a pleasant one," Semeli continued, "you have but to ask and I shall see that it is provided." Her eyes hardened a little. "As my duties allow."

He knew what she meant. Creature comforts she would do her best to provide, but if he had any notion that she was willing to do what some men demanded of their female servants—at night—she would not comply.

"I understand," he said.

Another young woman stepped out from behind some of the men. She was very pretty, with long, honey-colored hair, and a very exceptional figure. "I'm Moll," she said with a bright smile as she twisted a lock of her thick hair about her finger, "and if you need anything, my lord, *anything at all*, you can ask me."

He nearly laughed out loud at her astonishingly brazen invitation. Obviously, unlike Semeli, she was willing to do whatever a squire requested.

"Moll works in the kitchen," Lady Gwyneth snapped. "And she should be there now, shouldn't you, Moll?"

Moll stopped smiling and acting coy. "Yes, my lady," she murmured. She bowed and turned to go, pausing to flash him another brilliant smile.

Moll was no Lady Gwyneth, of course, but he was no squire, and the maidservant's offer was definitely flattering.

Lady Gwyneth grabbed his arm and tugged him toward another young man who had arms the size of small tree trunks. His round face was streaked with soot, making his light blue eyes look out of place.

"Gavin, this is Darton, the smith's son. He's quite good with a quarter staff," she said, sounding distinctly annoyed.

Obviously she didn't appreciate Moll's bold behavior, which seemed a little odd, considering how bold she herself could be.

As for Darton and his quarter staff, he could believe

the young man would be a menace with that simple weapon. His arms were so muscular, the fellow could probably kill an opponent with a single well-aimed blow of the slender pole.

The next young man seemed about to jump out of his skin, for he bobbed and twitched and grinned and frowned until Gavin wondered if he was mad. "Gavin of Inverlea, this is Emlyn."

"Pleased to meet you, my lord, sir," Emlyn said eagerly, his green eyes wide with excitement. He was very thin, and his hair was as black as coal. "I'm the miller's apprentice, me."

"You're Welsh?" Gavin guessed.

"Aye, I am, I am, like our noble lady's sainted mother!" Emlyn cried, smiling. "My father came here with her when she married the earl. So I am a fine shot with a bow, and I'll be happy to show any others. Nobody shoots like the Welsh, do they?"

Skill with a bow might come in handy for him, too, so with a genuine smile, Gavin said, "I hope you'll teach me, too."

The lad's mouth fell open, and immediately Gavin realized he had made a mistake. Noblemen didn't use bows. Such weapons were considered suitable only for foot soldiers and peasants.

"I think a nobleman should at least know how the

weapons work, don't you?" he said quickly. "I would never use one in battle myself, however."

Lady Gwyneth laughed, but he heard the tension in it.

He decided to say as little as possible from then on, to the men as well as the women. He stayed silent as Gwyneth continued the introductions, telling him about each man and what he did, and then the rest of the servants of the household. It became clear that every one of them both liked and respected their young mistress.

He wondered how Lady Gwyneth managed to provide for them all, until he considered that the tithes the farmers on the estate paid would ensure enough food for the castle household, at least to survive, even in lean years. The earl would need more than enough to merely survive, though, if he was to pay his taxes and keep a garrison. The difference between the income from the tithes and the taxes he owed the Crown could, Gavin supposed, lead to poverty.

The introductions completed at last, they started toward the hall. "I have invited all the men to eat with us," Lady Gwyneth remarked.

It took a great effort for him to keep walking. "They'll see me eat."

She gave him an unsympathetic look. "Do as you did in the chapel and imitate me. If you were willing to risk your immortal soul taking the holy bread, surely you can risk making a mistake of etiquette. Besides, everybody thinks you are a Scot. As long as you don't eat from the plate like a dog, you'll do all right."

Gavin wasn't so sure, but he wasn't about to admit it.

CHAPTER SIX

Gwyneth watched Gavin out of the corner of her eye while she wiped her fingers on the plain white napkin prior to the start of the meal. They were seated together at the high table on the dais, far enough away from the rest of the people in the hall that they could not be heard if they spoke softly. That was good because she had things to say to him she didn't want anybody to overhear.

Following her example, Gavin dipped his fingers in the shallow basin to clean them, then dried them. As he did, he shot her a scornful glance. "Seems a waste of clean water to me," he muttered.

"It's what a squire would do."

"If you say so."

"I do."

As he resumed his sullen silence, Gwyneth was forced to concede, if only to herself, that she was not as prepared as she should have been. She should have expected Thomas's questions and had answers ready. She should have kept her temper better at Moll's brazen behavior, even if she hadn't foreseen it. As for Gavin's taking the host— who could have guessed he would put his immortal soul in peril to maintain a ruse?

She slid Gavin a sidelong glance as he pulled at the knot of the lacing of his white shirt until it came undone. He sighed as he loosened the ties, exposing his chest more than good taste allowed.

He really was an uncivilized lout. A handsome, strong, uncivilized lout who had to learn from his mistakes. "You should not have taken the bread at mass."

"It seemed the proper thing to do," he replied, mimicking her haughty tone.

"If you want to put your soul in danger," she retorted, hurt by his mockery more than she cared to admit.

"It already is, and I thought it best to do *everything* you did." He shifted in his chair. "How the devil do you sit with your back against this thing?"

"For one thing, you don't slouch. Or wriggle. One would think you hadn't sat in a chair before."

"I haven't, not that I can remember, anyway—only benches or the ground. I don't like being on the dais like this, either. I feel like a trained bear. I expect somebody to make me dance."

"I suppose it must be difficult when you're not used to it, but if you don't sit still, everyone will wonder why not."

"Tell them I have an itchy rash or some such thing."

"I will not lie more than I have to, Gavin. Surely you can sit still. Even little children can."

"Little noble children, maybe."

"I'm not going to argue about this."

Gavin frowned. "Oh, very well. I'll try to sit still and not do anything without your leave or example." He lowered his voice even more. "You should have warned me about your reeve. He's suspicious. I thought you said nobody would question what you told them."

He was right. She *should* have warned him about Thomas, the one person who would not automatically believe her. It was said he trusted no woman at all, and never had after hearing about Eve and the apple.

At least Thomas wasn't in the hall now. He had left the courtyard to attend to his daily duties. "Thomas is suspicious of everybody. I will deal with him."

She gave Gavin another condemning glance, for she was not the only one who had made mistakes this morning. "We should have decided who you served before you came out with Sir Henry D'Argent."

Gavin's eyes gleamed with annoyance. "I was doing my best."

"He's the most famous knight in the realm. Why didn't you just say you were the king's squire?" she asked sarcastically, her frustration growing.

"Of course I know Sir Henry D'Argent is famous. Why do you think his name came to me first? Would you rather I said something like Sir Swine of Swampton?"

She made a pert little grimace of acknowledgment.

"Very well, we should have discussed some of these things before you met Thomas."

"We? This isn't my plan. And what about Inverlea? Is that a real place? If it is, you'd better tell me about it, or I'm liable to say it has a cathedral when it doesn't, or some such thing."

"I made it up, and you will stop addressing me in that impertinent manner. I am well aware whose plan this is and I have agreed I made an error by not expecting all of the questions you might be asked. We have *both* made mistakes today. However, if you will simply do as you're told and follow my lead, we should succeed."

"Act like your dog, in other words." Gavin nodded at Rufus sitting beside her, waiting patiently for any morsel of food that might fall into the rushes.

"You have certainly learned to act as arrogantly as any squire," she retorted, her voice low and stern. "And stay away from the female servants."

"Even Moll? She seemed very friendly."

"Yes, even Moll," she snapped. Moll chased anything in breeches, but she would not have the girl believe she was offering her favors to a nobleman.

Gavin grinned at her, a mischievous, knowing, devilish grin. "Why, my lady, I believe you're jealous."

She flushed hotly. "I am not!"

"Yes, you are."

He was so very sure of himself! "No, I'm not!"

"I like girls with spirit, but that Moll's too bold for my taste."

What did he think about *her*? Was she too bold, too?

Such thoughts were utterly ridiculous, and so was his stupid notion. "I am not jealous of Moll. The very idea is laughable. She's a brazen hussy and a serving wench. I'm Lady Gwyneth of Haverleigh, and as the lady of Haverleigh, I command you to leave Moll alone."

"You'd do better to tell her to leave *me* alone."

"Perhaps I will."

"You should."

"Fine."

"Fine."

This quarrel had gone on long enough. If they argued anymore, she was sure to raise her voice, and that would never do. Everyone must think they were at least friendly, or why would the squire stay?

"Is your father going to join us?" Gavin asked after a moment, startling her.

"He is too ill to leave his chamber at present."

The instant the words were out of her mouth, she wanted to call them back. She should not let him know how sick her father was, for that might make him think her vulnerable.

Instead of asking more questions, however, Gavin sniffed the air wafting in from the corridor leading to the kitchen, which for safety's sake was not a part of the hall.

A delighted smile lit his face. "Fresh bread."

She nodded, and secretly admitted that the aroma *was* wonderful. Then she wondered if she should tell him not to look quite so thrilled by the prospect of a loaf of bread.

She didn't because the serving women, Moll among them, entered the hall from the kitchen corridor. Each carried a basket of bread or cheese. Gavin stared at them so hard, it wasn't difficult to believe he was looking at the girl, not what she carried.

Maybe he was, and so what of that? The notion that a squire would find a serving girl interesting, at least in one way, was an explanation for his behavior everyone would accept, and she should be pleased by that.

Moll sauntered toward the high table, her basket of bread balanced on her hip. She looked at Gavin boldly and smiled as she set the basket in front of him.

Gwyneth clenched her teeth.

His hand reached for the bread.

She grabbed his knee beneath the table. He shouldn't eat yet, not until he crossed himself!

Startled, he hesitated and looked at her, his eyes wide.

She said nothing while she just as quickly withdrew her hand, then crossed herself. She waited for him to do the same. Mercifully he did, without any more prodding from her.

Moll next brought them some cheese, and poured ale into their mazurs, wide wooden cups with metal brims. She did all with the same saucy impertinence, giving Gavin coy looks and smiles. Gwyneth got more and more annoyed at her, at him, and at herself, because she couldn't *stop* being annoyed, until she realized Moll was being so brazen because Gavin was ignoring her. Although he wasn't wolfing down his food like a starving man, he was certainly giving it his full attention.

Gwyneth was suddenly quite hungry herself, and ate heartily.

"'Ere now, my chick," the middle-aged Peg declared as she went by the table and eyed her. "Don't be eating so fast, or you'll be belching all day long."

Gwyneth flushed. Sometimes Peg could be a little too familiar. She was a lady, after all, and nearly sixteen years old—too old to be scolded like a child.

It didn't make her feel any better to notice the hint of a smile curving Gavin's lips as he reached for a drink of ale, the beverage served at all meals. Nobles usually had wine, but now they reserved it for special occasions, such as when the baron paid an unwelcome visit.

She wouldn't look at Gavin anymore, she decided, until the meal was done. That was all too soon, because the food was simple: bread and cheese and ale.

She realized that Gavin was watching her. There was not a crumb left in front of him, so he couldn't be looking to her for direction on how to eat. "What is it?" she mumbled under her breath.

"Where is the rest of it?" he whispered.

"The rest of what?"

"The food. Surely this can't be all."

She didn't enjoy being reminded how meager their fare was these days. "Of course it is."

His brow furrowed with puzzlement. "How are the men supposed to train with so little in their bellies?"

"Normally we don't eat even this much before noon, but I thought all the men should have something before the training begins. Otherwise, eating before midday is only for the very young, the sick, or the old—not grown men or youths."

"Grown men who don't have much work to do could hold out until then, I suppose—noblemen and the like, who sit idly by while others till their land and defend it, too."

"It is the way of things."

"It is a stupid way."

"Even if I agreed with you—and I don't—there is no help for it. We cannot feed this many every morning."

"So let them come after they have broken the fast at home, or after the midday meal, when they have done their work for the day."

"Then they will be too tired to learn properly."

"It is their work that provides for you, my lady."

"It is this castle that protects them."

"It is the *soldiers* in this castle who defend you and your estate. They protect you as much as the stone walls. If these tenants are to be soldiers, too, you should value them and their work all the more. Besides, they will learn because they know as well as you do how important defending Haverleigh is. Men fight hardest when they're defending their homes."

Although he was helping her, he still had no right to talk to her this way. It wasn't as if he really was a squire, and so of equal rank with her. "You seem to forget to whom you are speaking, Gavin. And have you suddenly become an expert on what makes men good soldiers?"

He flushed, but he didn't look sorry. "I know what makes men fight. If they are tired when they learn, so be it—but they will fight harder than any paid foot soldier when the time comes because this is their home."

He had a good point, and she shouldn't disagree just because his manner annoyed her. "Very well, then. In future, they may come after midday."

He reached out and covered her hand with his, the sudden action as well as the warmth of his palm surprising her. "A wise decision, my lady."

She knew she should pull her hand out from under his. She knew she shouldn't let him touch her. She also knew it was a sin to enjoy it.

"Are we going to learn how to fight, or are you two going to play patty fingers all morning?" Hollis called out, a wide grin slashing his face.

Gwyneth burned with embarrassment, as if she were sitting in the middle of a blazing hearth in midsummer. She jumped to her feet and opened her mouth to say something, anything—but before she could, Gavin rose and glared at her friend. "You dare to speak so to the lady of Haverleigh?"

Hollis stopped grinning.

"Hollis and I used to play together as children, so there's no need to be so fierce."

Ignoring her, Gavin marched toward her friend. Hollis went so pale, his freckles looked like plague spots.

Gavin grabbed him by his tunic and hauled him to his feet. "Well, Hollis," he growled as he let go and Hollis righted himself, "what do you have to say for yourself?"

"I . . . that is, Lady Gwyneth and I . . ." he stammered as Gwyneth hurried toward them.

"There is no need for that!" she cried as she came to a halt beside Hollis. "Hollis and I are old friends."

"And that allows him to talk to you in that insolent way?"

No matter how majestic and regally angry Gavin sounded, he was still just a peasant and a thief. How dare he frighten her friend like that? "Yes, it does. I take no offense, and neither should you. However, I shall take great offense if you hurt him."

"He's not hurt, are you, Hollis?"

"No, no, I'm fine."

Apparently satisfied, Gavin made a brisk little bow to Gwyneth. "The last thing I want to do is offend you, my lady, so his impertinence will be forgotten." He glanced sharply at Hollis. "*This* time. Now, my lady, if you will be so good as to show me where I am to begin the training?"

He smiled so unexpectedly, she felt as if he had hauled *her* to her feet and abruptly let her go. Then he held out his arm to her, as if nothing at all had happened.

Since the meal was finished, she had little choice but to let him lead her out of the hall, Rufus trotting obediently behind.

Her rather stunned and shocked state lasted only until she realized nobody was close by in the courtyard.

She pulled Gavin to a stop. Facing him, she put her hands on her hips and demanded, "What was that all about? Why were you so harsh with Hollis?"

His calm smile infuriated her. "I was acting like a squire."

"You have no right to . . . to . . ."

"Act like a squire? You would rather I ignored your friend's joke about 'patty fingers'? Do you think a real squire would have?"

She lifted her chin defiantly. "He might have—and there was no reason for you to grab Hollis like that. You acted like a . . . like a *ruffian!*"

His lips curved just enough to unnerve her again and

she fought to regain her self-control. "That's what I am, my lady, and he was more surprised than hurt."

"Whether he was hurt or not," she retorted, trying to maintain her indignation despite his smile, "you're *supposed* to be a squire—a gentleman."

"No squire I've ever seen would let a peasant like Hollis make such a joke and not be angry about it. Don't you see it was a sort of test? They know they can joke with you, and they wondered if they could do the same with me." His lips twisted into something that was not a smile, nor yet a frown. "If I had ever tried to jest with Fulk when he was teaching me how to steal, he would have beaten me. A teacher is not a friend, my lady, any more than a squire is the same as a peasant. Your men must respect me."

He had made another good point, but she still wasn't about to excuse him. "You didn't have to manhandle him like that, did you?"

He shrugged his broad shoulders. "Maybe not. I am new to this business of being a squire and a teacher, so perhaps I acted more angry than I had to."

She started toward the gate again. "You certainly did."

He hurried to catch up to her, his long legs making that easy. "You were more upset with Hollis than I was, though."

"I was not!"

"I saw it in your face."

Once more she halted, and she crossed her arms as she glared at him. "You were wrong to hold my hand like that."

His smile was pure devilment, as if what he had done was nothing more than a joke, and again he bowed. "I humbly beg your forgiveness, my lady, and I won't do it again. Unless you ask me to."

Scowling, Lady Gwyneth turned on her heel and continued on her way.

CHAPTER SEVEN

As Gavin fell into step beside the indignant Gwyneth, he tried to master his frustration and take some pleasure from the way he held his own in the hall and then the courtyard.

He had been right to react to Hollis's remark about patty fingers as he had. A real squire would have been angry at the fellow's impertinence.

She had been flustered when he'd taken her hand, too, try as she might to hide it, just as she'd tried to deny that she was upset by Moll's obvious interest in him.

If Lady Gwyneth cared enough to be jealous, she might be a little weak where he was concerned. He could use that weakness to his advantage.

He had to admit he enjoyed being with her, even when they quarreled. . . . maybe *especially* when they quarreled. He liked seeing the fierce, bold sparkle of her blue eyes, the way her lips tightened ever so slightly, the little thrust of her proud chin.

He wondered what she would do if he ever tried to kiss her.

Lady Gwyneth glanced back over her shoulder. "Don't

dawdle. The others are coming."

Distracted by the notion of kissing her, he obediently quickened his pace. "Where are we going?"

"The river meadow," she replied bluntly, obviously in no mood to talk to him anymore.

Well, so be it. He should pay attention to his surroundings anyway, in case he had to flee.

They passed through the gatehouse and went on through the small village that clustered about the protective walls of Haverleigh, on the other side of the ditch that served as a dry moat. Some alleys led off from the main road. Down one, he could make out what must be the smithy from the sounds of hammers banging on iron anvils. Nearby was a larger two story building, with a low wall around it that looked like a stable. It was probably an inn.

They came to the village green, a more open space where the market was. A tall oak shaded one part of it, and there were a few stalls with food and household items for sale.

There were not as many stalls as he would have expected, and the people buying looked poor, too. Haverleigh was obviously not very prosperous.

There was one good thing about that: Fulk and the others wouldn't come here again, for the pickings would be too slim to make it worth their while.

After they walked a bit more, he saw a broad open expanse nearly two acres across, mostly flat, and without high grass. The sheep grazing there explained that. At the far end was a row of willows, telling him that was probably the riverbank.

She came to a halt and gestured at her big dog, who sat beside her.

"What do you intend to do first?" she asked Gavin.

As he looked back at the men and youths coming behind them, he started to sweat. He had never taught anybody anything, let alone while he was pretending to be something he was not. "What do you think I should do?"

"I have no idea."

"But you must have some!"

"No. I've never trained men—only Rufus."

"You did a fine job with him. How did you start?"

"I watched him being born."

In his desperation, Gavin forgot she was a lady and rolled his eyes. "That's not going to help me."

"I'm sure you'll think of something."

"I'm not! They'll know . . ." He fell silent.

"No, they won't. Unless you do something utterly stupid, you should be all right."

Not the most encouraging of remarks, but her words made him feel somewhat better nonetheless. Then she turned back toward the castle.

"Are you leaving?" he demanded, feeling as if he'd been cut adrift to be lost at sea.

"It wouldn't be right for me to stay." She gave him an unexpectedly friendly smile. "I know how hard it is to pretend you're not afraid when you really are."

"I'm not afraid!" he protested, although he couldn't help wondering if this was how you felt when your neck was about to be put in the noose.

Her eyes sparkled with warmth, and what looked suspiciously like triumph. "Besides, you've already let them know you are not to be trifled with, haven't you?"

With that, she walked away, her dog at her heels.

Well, he didn't need her help, Gavin told himself. It wasn't as if he hadn't been in tricky situations before.

The men and boys he was supposed to train gathered about him in a semicircle, waiting expectantly. If he had seen suspicion in their faces of the sort Thomas had displayed, he would have turned and fled like a condemned outlaw.

He didn't see suspicion or mistrust. Every man and youth there regarded him with what appeared to be respectful anticipation.

They believed the lie, and seeing that, Gavin's confidence returned.

"Now that I've met you, I'll do my best to remember your names," he declared, straightening his shoulders, "and teach you all I can. I think we'll start with . . ." He realized not a one of them was armed, and he only had the knife hidden in his breeches. "Don't any of you have weapons?"

The men and boys glanced at one another uneasily.

"I've got my bow," Emlyn declared, fairly leaping forward and unslinging it from around his chest. "And arrows, too." He patted the quiver hanging from his belt.

"Anybody else?"

"We don't own any," said a middle-aged man who looked every inch a farmer in his mended woolens. "His lordship keeps 'em in the armory."

"It's Fenwick, isn't it?"

"Aye, sir," the man answered with a smile that exposed his few remaining teeth. "The swords and spears and things, they'd be in the armory back at the castle."

"Of course. I should have asked Lady Gwyneth about weapons. Well, no matter. You should know how to fight without weapons, too. In a real fight—battle," he amended, remembering he was supposed to be a squire and not a tavern brawler, "they can get knocked from your hands."

The men nodded approvingly. Encouraged, Gavin removed his tunic and shirt, then folded them and set them carefully on the grass.

They were staring at him. "I am going to teach you fighting, not dancing, and I don't want to ruin the fine clothes your lady gave me because mine were stolen. You men can leave yours on if you like. It will give me more to grab to throw you down, though," he warned. "Now, I'll try you one at a time. Who's first?"

The men and youths exchanged wary glances.

"Have no fear. I won't complain if you best me, or give me a few bruises. I've had plenty in my time."

"I will try!" Hollis eagerly stepped forward and tore off his tunic. Half naked, he was as pale and skinny as a plucked chicken.

"Very well." Making fists and holding them up in front of his chin, Gavin crouched low and started to sway. Hollis imitated him, although it was clear the fellow really had no idea what he was doing, or why.

"You want to guard your face, Hollis. And a moving target is harder to hit," he explained.

He looked just to the right of Hollis, as if there was something in the grass. He kept his gaze on that spot even as Hollis started to sidle closer. Finally, Hollis glanced down to see what was so fascinating. In that instant, Gavin rushed him, shoving him to the ground. As Hollis looked up, stunned and surprised, Gavin placed his foot on his throat.

"And that, I fear, would be the end of you," he said as he removed his foot and held out his hand to help Hollis up.

"God's blood," Hollis muttered as he got to his feet, rubbing his throat. Then he grinned widely. "I thought there must be a snake or something at my feet."

"That's the idea," Gavin replied, pleased that there were no hard feelings. These people didn't have to like him, but he didn't want them to hate him, either.

He scanned the gathering, secretly delighted to see respect and awe in the faces of the men, both young and old. "Who's next?"

The energetic Emlyn fairly leaped forward. "Me! I won't fall for that trick. But remember I'm an archer, not a bloody wrestler, so have a care of my fingers."

"Then knock me down," Gavin genially suggested.

Emlyn didn't fall for the snake-in-the-grass trick, but he had no idea how to protect his face with his fists, or block a blow, so one swift punch to his chin quickly had him flat on his back.

Again, Gavin held out his hand to his fallen foe. "You've got to keep your hands up until you strike," he said as Emlyn scrambled to his feet.

"I'm an archer, I am," the defeated youth muttered, as he gathered up his bow and quiver of arrows, "not a bloody foot soldier!"

With that, he stomped off toward the riverbank, where he threw down his bow and arrows, then sat and stared out at the water flowing between the trees.

"A sulky one, our Emlyn," Fenwick offered with a smile. "He'll come 'round by the time we eat." His smile grew. "So, Gavin of Inverlea, you've tried a couple of boys, how 'bout a man now, eh?"

The men of Haverleigh quickly learned that neither age nor size mattered much to Gavin. One by one they fell to the ground, at Gavin's mercy, then joined the ranks of the defeated who watched and cheered. Eventually, even Emlyn stopped sulking and came to watch his fellows.

As far as their fighting abilities, Gavin saw much to be pleased about. With a little training and a few tricks, they should all be able to hold their own.

Finally, panting, sweating, bent over with his hands on his knees, Gavin raised his head to survey the men and boys laughing and shouting consoling encouragement to their latest companion to fall, a rather thin shepherd who rolled over and stood up, wiping the trickle of blood from his nose where Gavin had punched him. Thank God he was the last, Gavin thought wearily.

At least here, though, he felt comfortable and confident. In the hall, it was as if he was in a foreign land where he didn't know the customs or the language. But fighting and protecting himself—that he knew.

"I'm not too late, I hope!"

Gavin looked up the road leading to the village and wanted to groan aloud. Darton, the blacksmith's son, lumbered toward them as if the village were on fire.

"I had t' stay and shoe a horse, but I come as soon as I could," he said by way of explanation as he halted and started to peel off his leather apron.

"Not too late, am I? I like a bit o' fightin'." His white

teeth gleaming nearly as brightly as his eyes, he regarded Gavin eagerly.

Gavin straightened, ready to tell them it was too late in the day, to say nothing of how tired he was, when he saw Lady Gwyneth approaching, Semeli beside her.

Had she come to see if he had survived, or at least managed to keep up the ruse?

Angered by that thought, his pride wounded, he gave Darton a nod of agreement and began to circle the smith's son. "Right, then. Let's go."

Big and brawny probably meant slow, and Darton's size could be used against him, if Gavin could only get him off balance.

Unfortunately, he quickly discovered that Darton was as quick as a dancer on a feast day, and he hadn't been joking when he said he liked a good fight. Not even breaking a sweat, he didn't stop smiling as Gavin tried every trick, every feint, every move he knew to knock his opponent down, all to no avail.

Around them the other men stood in a circle, watching and whispering. He heard enough to know that wagers were being made, and that he was expected to lose, which didn't help matters. Lady Gwyneth and Semeli were there somewhere, too, but he didn't dare look for them as he wondered when the big ox was going to strike.

Before he could even blink, Darton's arm shot out like

a serpent, hitting him right in the nose, just as he'd hit the shepherd. He found himself looking up at the sky, his nose throbbing with excruciating pain, and he could taste his blood on his lips.

Lady Gwyneth came into view, looking down at him, her face full of concern. "Are you hurt?"

Gavin felt his nose, wincing at the pain and trying not to. He wiped the blood from under it with the back of his hand. "It's not broken, is it?" he asked.

She squatted down beside him and brushed his hair back from his forehead. "I think not."

"I barely touched 'im," Darton said as he loomed over him, blocking out the sky. "Just a tap, it were."

"I know," Lady Gwyneth said with more sympathy for the smith than she had shown when she'd spoken to him.

On the other hand, she wasn't brushing Darton's hair from his forehead.

"If that's your idea of a tap, remind me never to make you angry," Gavin said as he splayed his hands on the grass behind him and eased himself to a sitting position.

"Darton's the bare-knuckle fighting champion of three shires," Lady Gwyneth calmly remarked.

"Fine time to find out," Gavin muttered as he got to his feet.

Suddenly mindful of his bare chest, he reached down for his shirt. A stab of pain between his eyes caused them to water and his nose throbbed, but he made no sound at all. He wouldn't, not while he was the center of attention.

He drew on his shirt and glared at the men. "Somebody might have told me about him."

"You didn't ask if any o' us could fight," Fenwick said, "or I would 'ave told ya about Darton. He's the pride and joy o' Haverleigh, he is, savin' her ladyship 'ere."

Deciding it wouldn't do any good to be angry at them, Gavin put on the tunic, careful that there was no blood left on his face to ruin it as he pulled it over his head. "We're finished for today," he announced. "We'll meet here again after the noon tomorrow."

With smiles and farewells, the men began to leave the field, all except Hollis, who lingered by the road with Semeli.

"So, how did they do?" Lady Gwyneth asked quietly.

"Well enough," Gavin growled, "but if there's anybody else who's the bare-knuckle fighting champion of three shires, or two or one, I wish you'd tell me now."

"No, just Darton." Lady Gwyneth didn't meet his angry gaze. "And you're right. I should have told you that, too."

"You should also tell me what weapons you have, and anything else I should rightly know if I am to be Gavin of Inverlea training your men. You should be helping me, not enjoying my shame as if I were some sort of jester meant to amuse you."

"I wasn't enjoying your shame."

"You certainly didn't seem too upset to see me flat on

my back with a bloody nose."

She flushed. "What did you want me to do? Clean your face for you?"

Determined to tip the balance in his favor, Gavin resorted to her apparent attraction to him. "You did before, didn't you? And combed my hair."

She raised her chin defiantly. "Yes, I washed your face. It was filthy. I also combed your hair—and a hard time I had. It was like a rat's nest."

So much for tipping the balance in his favor. His face felt hot, and he guessed he was blushing.

Hollis left Semeli and approached them. Running his hand through his hair until it stuck up even more, he said, "I want to apologize, my lady. I spoke out of turn there in the hall. I hope you're not angry."

"No, I'm not, Hollis."

He grinned with relief. "That's good." He turned to Gavin. "And I won't be saying nothing like that again, my lord."

"See that you don't."

"Good day, Hollis." Lady Gwyneth began to walk toward the castle, then turned and looked at Gavin, obviously expecting him to trot along after her just as Rufus was doing. Subduing a scowl, he did, while Hollis and Semeli followed a short distance behind.

"I suppose I should warn you about Emlyn. He sulks," she remarked.

Gavin was in no mood to mince words. "I found that out for myself."

"Oh." She slid him a sidelong glance. "He's really very good with a bow. He took a prize at the fair last May Day."

"If you say so." Gavin changed the subject to something more important. "The men don't have any weapons, except Emlyn, with his bow. They said they would be in the armory."

"Yes, that's true. I can take you there now, if you like. I haven't had to sell any of the weapons yet."

If *he* liked? What had anything here to do with what *he* liked?

CHAPTER EIGHT

Gwyneth led Gavin through the gatehouse and across the cobblestoned courtyard toward a large stone building beside the stable. Her dog trotted off toward the kitchen, and as Rufus entered it, Moll appeared at the door.

Gavin smiled and gave her a little bow. Maybe a squire would do that, and maybe he wouldn't. To listen to some servants talk in a tavern, young noblemen spent far more time questing after pretty girls than after knightly honor, so why not?

They came to a halt outside the stone building. Lady Gwyneth took a heavy iron key from the ring she wore at her waist and slipped it into an equally large iron lock. No quick twist of the knife would work that, he guessed, as she turned the key and pushed open the thick oaken door.

Inside, it was dark, save for the dim light that came in through the door. Gwyneth quickly and easily found a pair of flints, then proceeded to light a torch, which she stuck in a bracket on the wall.

As he looked around, he let out a low whistle. "Now I know why that key's so big."

He had never seen so many weapons in one place in

his life. There were racks of swords along one wall and several long spears leaned against the opposite one, their points gleaming dully. Bows also leaned against the wall. Quivers of arrows lay on wooden shelves beside them. "You don't seem so very poor now," he muttered.

"We can't eat swords or spears. I have barely a coin to my name, and while I may yet have things to sell, I dare not sell the weapons. We need them for protection. Surely even a thief can understand that."

His mouth a grim line, Gavin wheeled around and strode to one of the sword racks.

Gwyneth told herself she didn't care if he was angry. He was forgetting who he was, and his only purpose here. He seemed to think he really was a squire. He was acting proud and haughty and he flirted with the servants.

Gavin chose a sword, then moved into the open area in the center of the armory. He crouched and swung it as if there were an invisible opponent opposite him.

Despite how he angered her, she couldn't help admiring the easy way he moved. She had seen only a few men with that athletic grace, a way of moving as if their bodies were a part of the weapon itself.

She remembered how he looked without his shirt or tunic on, and suddenly her throat was very dry. "You shouldn't walk about half naked," she blurted.

His head snapped around with surprise.

She almost clapped her hand over her mouth. How she wished she had kept silent!

His brows lowered. "I took my shirt and tunic off so I wouldn't get them dirty with mud or sweat. If that offends your notion of proper behavior, my lady, I shall keep my clothes on at all times. But if I stink to high heaven, you can't tell me I offend you with the stench."

"You're supposed to be a squire," she reminded him. "Squires don't strut like barechested peacocks."

"I am supposed to be training your men, too. If you don't like how I do it, let me go."

"No. Not until they have learned how to fight."

"With all their clothes on."

"Yes!"

Scowling, he put back the sword, then gestured at the bows. "Emlyn sees himself at the head of a great troop of archers. How many bows are there?"

"I don't know. Count them."

His eyes flashed with anger as he leaned back against a bare space in the wall. He crossed his arms and his ankles. "I can't count past twenty."

His declaration sounded more like a challenge than an explanation.

She studied him a moment, her annoyance increased by his insolent attitude. "You don't know how to read, either, I expect."

"Not a word," he freely admitted. "Do you think you should teach me how to read, too, my lady?"

She immediately pictured herself sitting beside him, their faces so close together they almost touched as they bent over a scroll, his slender finger tracing a letter . . .

By all the blessed saints, what a thought!

Gavin pushed himself off the wall and walked toward her.

She should back away. No, she should stand her ground. She was Lady Gwyneth of Haverleigh . . . who was alone with this insolent and very handsome young man.

She moved back, the blood throbbing in her temples and her heart racing. "I can't teach you how to read!"

At the gleam of triumph in his eyes, she forced herself to become calmer—or at least, act it. She wouldn't let him get the upper hand, not here or anywhere, no matter what the circumstances. Not even if he was handsome and exciting and so very different from any boy she had ever met. "It would look strange. A squire should already know how to read."

He smiled. Slowly. As if he knew his very presence was disturbing to her, and that pleased him. "Too bad." He strolled a little closer. "Maybe there are some things *I* can teach *you*."

She scurried to the opposite wall. "Don't you come near me!"

Laughing softly, a smug look on his face, Gavin

made a mocking bow. "Fear not, my lady. I know I am not worthy to touch the hem of your gown, so your honor is safe. Nor shall I touch you—unless you want me to. Do you want me to?"

Ashamed of fleeing across the room, and her pride roused by his impertinence, she planted her feet and glared at him. "You rude, insolent—"

"What?" he demanded, marching toward her and halting a foot in front of her. "Rude, insolent lackey? Rude, insolent, false squire? Rude, insolent thief not fit to wipe your boots?"

He sidled closer. "Rude, insolent fellow you *need*?"

Excitement vibrantly trembled through her, a feeling heady and wondrous, and new and unfamiliar.

And dangerous?

She would ignore it and face him down. "Once again you forget to whom you are speaking, Gavin."

"I know very well who I'm talking to, my lady."

She would ignore the warmth flooding through her as he studied her as if he had never really looked at her before.

The torch started to splutter and the light dimmed, but neither of them moved.

Transfixed by the rapid rising and falling of his chest, she could scarcely breathe herself.

The torch flickered once. Twice.

His expression changed again. His fiercely passionate

anger seemed to tremble and shift, to rearrange itself into another kind of passion, something yearning and uncertain, vulnerable and incredibly intense.

He reached out and pulled her into his arms.

Then his lips found hers.

All her anger and annoyance and frustration and fears fled like so much dust in the wind. The soft, simple brush of his mouth across hers was like the most beautiful, thrilling compliment.

She had never been kissed before. She had never imagined that a kiss could be like this . . . sweet, tender, and yet making her feel incredibly alive.

The torch light went out. They were alone in the dark.

His embrace tightened, and his kiss deepened. His tongue pressed against her lips ever so slightly—but it was enough.

Enough to surprise her. Enough to shock her. Enough to remind her that this was wrong. They should not be here. Alone. Together. His arms about her, his lips on hers. She was a lady; he was a thief. She was the daughter of a lord, destined to marry into a noble family. He was outside the law and was probably going to end his days at the end of a rope.

She splayed her hands on his chest and pushed him away. How could she have done that? How could she have let him . . . let herself . . . ? Panting, she ran to the door and fumbled with the latch.

"My lady, I—"

She yanked open the door and hurried into the court-yard, afraid to look back. Afraid to see him right now, or to look into his dark eyes. And more afraid of her own weakness that made her forget who and what they were, and would always be.

She heard the dull thud as Gavin closed the door behind him. "You have to lock it," he called out.

Embarrassed and ashamed, she halted and quickly scanned the courtyard. Moll was near the well. Moll, of all people.

With her back straight, and trying to ignore the heat of the blush coloring her face, she turned and went past him, twisting so that no part of her body touched his. With trembling hands, she locked the armory door.

As he watched her angrily avoiding him, Gavin knew he should not have kissed her. He didn't know what had come over him.

Yes, he did. He had kissed her because of the fire burning in her eyes that kindled something exciting and thrilling within him that he had never felt before. He had kissed her because she was jealous of a serving girl who'd smiled at him. He had kissed her because as the yearning to kiss her had taken possession of him, her eyes had told him she felt that same attraction, that same need.

In this, at least, they were equals.

But, Gavin told himself, that was a foolish, ridiculous

notion, and kissing her had probably been the greatest mistake of his life.

She faced him again, her eyes glistening like shards of ice. "Shall we go to the hall?" she asked, her voice serene.

But as cold as iron in winter.

Baron DeVilliers pushed his silver goblet out of the way and leaned his elbows on the high table in his hall. The air was filled with the grunts and gobbling noises of the rough, battle-hardened mercenaries he had hired in the month since he had last visited Haverleigh and realized stubborn little Gwyneth wasn't going to give in easily.

He wasn't about to let some girl stand in his way. He wanted Haverleigh, and by God, he was going to get it, one way or another. For years he had been working to increase his holdings, whether by legal means or not, for that meant more power at court.

As for Gwyneth's refusal of his proposal, that only proved what a fool she was. He was handsome; he was certainly far wealthier than her father, thanks to the dowry his mother had brought his father; and Gwyneth could do a lot worse. She should be glad he desired her.

Lacing his fingers together, DeVilliers laid his chin on them and twisted his head to regard Thomas beside him. Like the men of his regular garrison, Thomas looked discomfited by the new hirelings.

Thomas was another fool, although not such a fool

as Gwyneth, for he had realized the ultimate future of Haverleigh. Thomas knew that the baron would eventually be the overlord and it would not be wise to make an enemy of him. Better indeed to try to win the future lord's friendship, if he could.

Thomas caught his eye and made a weak smile, obviously torn between dread at what the presence of such mercenaries meant to his own safety and his pleasure at being seated at a lord's table, an honor which by rights a man of his rank did not deserve. Tonight, however, pleased with his mercenaries and the thought that Haverleigh must soon be his, DeVilliers had decided to make the man feel honored. A simple enough thing, but it had impressed the dolt.

Thomas wiped his dripping chin with his napkin, then dunked his fingers in the bowl of water beside him and cleaned them. "Wonderful, my lord. That was wonderful."

The flames of the torches in the brackets above DeVilliers's head flickered and smoked, making it appear that the embroidered figures in the tapestries behind the dais were bending close to hear their master speak. "Since you are the reeve of Haverleigh, it is my honor to have you at my table. I am also pleased to think the earl of Haverleigh's health is improving."

"So they say, my lord."

DeVilliers waited for Thomas to continue, knowing he would.

"I am not nearly so sure it truly is so, and even if his health is improving, it's possible that he will fall ill again," Thomas said, his words rushing out as if he had been anxious to say them for days. "If he does, I fear he will be too weakened by his past illness to survive."

"How very unfortunate. We must hope he does not sicken again," DeVilliers murmured with an insincere smile. "How long before Lord William regains strength enough to run the estate as he should?"

"Weeks, I fear, my lord."

"Poor fellow. And in the meantime, young Lady Gwyneth continues to rule Haverleigh alone."

"Unless the king decides otherwise," Thomas pointed out.

"Yes, unless John orders her to marry so that Lord William has a capable son-in-law to help him."

"I wish King John would, and soon," Thomas said. "Haverleigh should be run by a man. By you, my lord," he added with another fawning smile.

DeVilliers inclined his head in approval of the sentiment. "Obviously, then, you would welcome a husband for Gwyneth and see to it that the tenants did likewise."

Thomas glanced at the mercenaries before answering. "Aye, my lord."

DeVilliers adjusted the cuff of his white shirt beneath his long black tunic. "What is this other thing of great importance you came to tell me? Naturally I intend to reward you for your trouble."

Thomas's small, dark eyes gleamed with greed. "As you know there is no garrison at Haverleigh because the men deserted for lack of pay."

DeVilliers did know, for he had paid them to go. That way, the lord of Haverleigh would need his help. "Yes, and your young lady persists in refusing my offer of aid."

"Lady Gwyneth is training her tenants to be soldiers."

DeVilliers burst out laughing. He had never heard anything so utterly ridiculous in all his life. "What, Lady Gwyneth imagines herself some kind of Amazon— a woman warrior? That I would like to see!"

"It is not the lady who is doing the training, but a squire we found stripped and robbed in the wood. He'd been attacked and his escort fled, and he says his master doesn't need him right away, so he's stayed to train the men for her. In gratitude, he claims. He's not bad, either. I've seen enough soldiers in my day to know."

Thomas quailed under DeVilliers's cold glare and slid another glance at the mercenaries. "N-not as good as your men, of course," he stammered, "but good. I thought as you did, my lord, so I decided to watch them yesterday. I was surprised how good they were. And the men like him. I-I thought you ought to know, if you didn't already."

DeVilliers's frown deepened. "This unknown squire is working a miracle, is he?"

"I'll just say this, my lord: the people of Haverleigh

love Lady Gwyneth like she's some sort of saint, so it wouldn't have been easy for you to ride into Haverleigh and lay claim to the lady and the land at the best of times. I'd think twice about it now, even with these soldiers you've got here. I tell you, he's a good teacher—and now they've got weapons they know how to use . . . well, I'd just think twice is all, my lord."

DeVilliers scowled. "Exactly who is this young man?"

"He says he's a squire in the service of Sir Henry D'Argent."

This revelation did not please the baron. If it had been almost any other knight's squire, he would have ridden to Haverleigh at once and sent the impudent cur on his way, by brute force, if necessary.

But D'Argent was not a man to cross. He was from a family very powerful at court, certainly far more powerful than DeVilliers was. Offend D'Argent, and the baron's own climb to power might suffer.

The baron shifted in his chair and once again brought his anger under control as he steepled his fingers. "Why have you come to warn me, Thomas? Out of concern for me? Or is it that you do not consider Lady Gwyneth some sort of saint, any more than I do?"

"No man should have to take orders from a *girl*," Thomas said. "Her father's too sick to run the estate, and I don't think he's going to get better, no matter what that fancy doctor from Salisbury says. I've seen too much sickness and death to believe that. Haverleigh needs a man to rule, my lord. A strong man. A rich man. A man like you. I'm tired of waiting for the earl to get better or King John to do something."

"Patience is a virtue, Thomas."

"I've been patient. And so have you, my lord," he added in a wheedling tone.

DeVilliers's eyes flickered in the torch light, and he did not disagree. "Which is why a clever man who sees the way it will be wastes no time proving his loyalty to his future overlord. I can appreciate such cleverness, Thomas, and reward it, too."

Thomas smiled again and leaned closer, as if they were now the best of friends. "May I ask, my lord, why you have added more soldiers to your garrison?"

"Obviously because I think I need them," DeVilliers snapped, deciding to put the reeve in his place.

The man flushed.

Then DeVilliers smiled and said, "What reward would you like for bringing me this interesting piece of news, Thomas?"

Thomas looked at him uncertainly.

"Come, come, Thomas, I am more than happy to reward you. Name what you would have, and so long as it is within the bounds of reason, you may have it."

"My stepson Hollis is a thorn in my side," Thomas blurted. "He always came between me and my wife when she was alive, for she loved the brat too well and spoiled him. He needed discipline and a firm hand, but she wouldn't see it, always letting him go off with his friends when there was work to be done. Now she is dead, so I want him out of my house and somewhere far off so I'll never have to see his insolent face and that damn red hair again."

"Well, well, well. That isn't what I was expecting." And it would certainly be one of the less expensive rewards he had ever handed out, which rendered it attractive. "Why don't you get rid of him yourself?"

"I'm doing the best I can to make him, but you can *order* him to leave."

And back up that order by force, if necessary. "I see. Very well. As you wish, so it shall be."

"My lord, what would you have me do in the meantime, about the training of the men, I mean?"

"Nothing." As much as it galled him, De Villiers knew full well he could not move openly against the earl of Haverleigh, even with his mercenaries, not so long as anyone friendly with D'Argent was involved and the earl yet lived. "Let Lady Gwyneth play her little games. Teaching those bumpkins to fight against trained soldiers will be useless, but if it comforts her, she may waste her time and theirs, and this squire's, too."

He eyed Thomas. "However, you might keep me informed of their progress from time to time, for which

I shall be very grateful. And generous. Do you understand me?"

"Yes, my lord. Thank you, my lord."

DeVilliers leaned back in his chair, and as his gaze roved over his hall, another thought came to him, one that caused his rage to boil up anew. But again he hid his anger as he regarded the reeve. "Tell me, Thomas, how do they get along, this squire and the young lady? So many squires like to woo young ladies only to brag of their conquests later. Is he of that sort?"

Thomas shook his head. "I'd have heard if he were. You know how women laze about and gossip of such things, and I keep my eyes and ears open. She's a proud one, too, so it'd take more than a pretty face and some smooth words to—"

The handsome and smoothly flattering DeVilliers cocked a brow and Thomas colored.

"She'll be a worthy wife for you, my lord," he continued humbly, "and I pray that day won't be too far off."

Once again DeVilliers smiled his cold, cruel smile. "I hope so, too, Thomas. I hope so, too."

CHAPTER NINE

The day had dawned far and mild—perfect weather for training, Gavin thought as he sauntered through the green and passed by the village well on the way to the river meadow. So far, the men were doing as well as he had ever hoped they would, and even somewhat better. They had learned quickly how to protect themselves in a fight, how to twist and feint and bob and weave, how to land a blow and throw their opponents if they got a chance. Swords had been a little difficult, but they were getting better, and the spears were easiest of all. He hadn't started with the bows yet, much to Emlyn's disgust, but at least the energetic Welshman grudgingly participated in the rest of the training. If all went well, soon they would try the bows.

A group of girls clustered at the village well drawing water, talking, and laughing. When they noticed him, they immediately fell silent. More than one turned a brilliant red as they all looked at the ground bashfully.

He nodded at the girls as he passed. "Good day."

There was more giggling and excited whispers. They thought him handsome. They thought him noble. They thought him quite amazing.

He smiled to himself. He could get used to this life, and those good opinions—so different from thief, beggar, pauper, cur, and a host of other, worse names he had been called all his life.

He couldn't help swaggering a bit more, until the girls' mothers and mistresses appeared and began shooing them back to work.

At least those girls seemed to appreciate him. After that day in the armory, Lady Gwyneth could barely tolerate his presence.

He hadn't touched her since that day, hadn't said anything even a little impertinent and had worked hard teaching her men all he knew about fighting. He had tried to imitate her regal manner and behave as a squire would. Unfortunately, he didn't know how successful he'd been because she never told him.

He didn't have any idea what she really thought of him, either.

He wouldn't worry about that, he told himself yet again. His sojourn here was only temporary, anyway. As soon as the men were trained, he would be on his way.

Despite this conviction and his resolve to quit this place, more than once he had considered apologizing, both for the kiss and for arguing with her. She was, after all, above him in rank, and she could turn against him at any time. Yet every time the words were on his lips, her stern, stiff demeanor made him hesitate.

But even if she was upset with him, she should take the trouble to watch the men from time to time, just to see how they were progressing. How else was she to know when his task was completed?

Still, if she was in no hurry to have him leave, he was in no particular hurry to go. It had been a long time since he had known exactly where he was going to sleep, and his bed had never been so fine and soft. Moreover, he didn't have to steal to survive, or face a beating if he hadn't robbed enough to support his fellow thieves.

He was also being treated with a respect he had never known or imagined in his life, and his fellow combatants seemed to like him, too. He was actually making friends. To be sure, he would have to leave them behind, but he had never had friends before.

How would his friends and those admiring girls feel if they found out who and what he really was, and that he had tricked them?

It wasn't hard to guess: they would feel cheated and betrayed. Although the ruse was all Lady Gwyneth's idea, they would surely blame him more than her.

He should leave before the truth came out, and then they need never know. Lady Gwyneth wouldn't be keen to tell them, for she had tricked them, too.

Most noblewomen probably wouldn't care two straws what their underlings thought of them, but he suspected she was different in that, too. As the days had passed, he had come to see how well liked and respected she was, no doubt because she treated all with a similar affection and respect. The older women of both village and hall seemed to think of her as almost a daughter, and she apparently enjoyed and encouraged such easy relations with her underlings.

It would be a terrible thing for her to lose their good opinion, more than it would be for him.

"Oh, my lord, there you be!"

He halted and turned to find Moll strolling toward him.

He bit back a curse. He had managed to avoid the brazen girl, only occasionally smiling at her from a distance, because he didn't need another quarrel with Lady Gwyneth.

"What is it?" he asked as she came to a stop close to him and smiled coyly, her hip thrust out as she rested a basket on it.

He imagined a fly caught in a spider's web felt this way.

"You're off to the meadow, then?" she asked.

"Yes."

She pouted, pushing her lips out in a way he was sure usually had great effect on males of all ages. "You ain't very civil, my lord. Just askin', I was."

He was supposed to be a chivalrous nobleman, so he made an elegant bow, just as Lady Gwyneth had taught him. "Forgive me for being so blunt."

Moll smiled. No doubt she was used to having young

men wrapped around her little finger. "Thinkin' deep thoughts, were you?"

Having one young woman trying to control him was quite enough—but Moll wasn't miles above him in rank and status. Moll was pretty and obviously interested. Lady Gwyneth, on the other hand, didn't want to have anything to do with him, even though he might be risking his life by staying here.

Maybe it was time he stopped worrying about having another quarrel with Lady Gwyneth.

He gave Moll a warm and friendly smile. "Perhaps I was, or perhaps I was merely thinking it is a fine day."

"You know, it ain't every day, fine or otherwise, we have a handsome young lord like you at Haverleigh."

He moved a little closer. "You flatter me."

She tilted her head and with her free hand, flipped a strand of thick honey-colored hair over her shoulder. "It's the truth."

"I wager you say that to all the squires."

"No, I don't."

She was putting on quite a demonstration of feminine wiles—and there was nothing honest about it, he realized as he looked into her eyes. Oh, she thought him attractive, no doubt. Other girls had, too. But there was no genuine affection, no excitement . . . nothing like the way Lady Gwyneth had looked at him in the armory before he'd kissed her.

In fact, deep down, what he saw in Moll's eyes looked suspiciously like greed. He had met girls like her before, poor girls willing to do anything to get out of their poverty, with no heed at all for their future. If they were lucky, they would merely be abandoned by their wealthy lovers and left penniless.

Suddenly he was tired of her coy games, and tired of his ruse, too, in spite of its advantages. He could not abandon the ruse yet, but he would be finished playing games with Moll. "You're very pretty, Moll, but you should find yourself a husband and not chase after young noblemen who will never, ever marry a girl like you."

Any more than a young noblewoman would ever marry anyone like him.

Moll straightened and stopped batting her eyelashes. "Are you planning on entering the priesthood?"

He almost laughed aloud at her question. "I assure you, nothing could be further from the truth."

"I do like you, my lord, and you are a handsome bloke. A girl could do a lot worse."

"Yes, she could—and so will you, if you keep this up."

Moll's eyes flashed with sudden ire. "It's Lady Gwyneth, ain't it? I got eyes. I seen the way you look at her. And I've seen the way she *don't* look at you. I wouldn't be wastin' my time sniffin' round her skirts if I was you. Baron DeVilliers's goin' to marry her, one way or another, and he won't let no snot-nosed squire take her away from him. He'll kill ya first."

Before he could say a word in response, she gasped and covered her mouth, horrified. "Forgive me!" she cried, backing away.

If he really was a squire, her words would indeed be cause for punishment, and therefore he could not, by rights, ignore them. "I will—this time," he said, just as he had to Hollis.

"Oh, thank you, thank you, sir!" she cried. She turned, stumbled, scrambled upright, and ran back to the castle as if she couldn't flee him fast enough.

The same way Lady Gwyneth had fled the armory after he had kissed her. He shook off that memory as he continued on his way, the beauty of the day destroyed.

Yet he had to be grateful to Moll. He had let himself be lulled into feeling some measure of security, believing that this ploy had little risk because it had gone well so far. Moll had forcefully reminded him that he would be a fool to be complacent. Just because DeVilliers had not come back did not mean he was not to be feared, and just because no one had questioned his identity didn't mean they never would.

Why hadn't the baron returned to Haverleigh? Maybe he was too busy running his own estate, which the men said was considerably larger than Haverleigh. Maybe he was sick. Maybe DeVilliers hadn't heard about the training. After all, who would tell him? The men of Haverleigh? Not likely, not when DeVilliers was the enemy. There had been no peddlers or other travelers passing through to carry the news.

Yes, that was probably the answer. DeVilliers was ignorant of what was happening at Haverleigh, and as long as DeVilliers stayed ignorant, he was safe enough—but only that long.

He should also not be so quick to think he was completely free of Fulk and the others, although it was easy to believe Fulk, Drogo, and Bert would have made their presence known if they were still around. They must have moved on. They probably thought he was dead.

No matter how comfortable he was here, though, and as tempting as it was to stay, he must never forget he was a thief, an outlaw, subject to the penalty of death if he was caught and his true identity revealed. He was not Gavin of Inverlea, squire to the most famous knight of the realm.

He was Gavin the thief, and he must be ready to flee at a moment's notice.

Rufus seated beside her, Gwyneth nervously clasped her hands as she watched the physician examine her father. James of Salisbury was reputed to be the most learned doctor outside of London. She tried to take some comfort in that, even though it seemed the middle-aged man's examination of her father would never end.

She told herself that was the only reason for the tension in her body, her shoulders, and her neck as she listened to James's questions and her father's answers. Well, that and Thomas's discontent. He made no secret of his continuing opposition to her plan to train the men. Every day, no matter what he came to discuss, whether it was rents or a tenant's tithe or days of service, he always brought the discussion around to Gavin and the training.

She didn't want to talk about Gavin more than she had to. She didn't want to think about him, either, but that was proving impossible, even when he wasn't nearby.

It was all because of what had happened in the armory, of course. His brazen, impudent action had made things difficult and awkward, and although he was doing a good job, according to Semeli, she could scarcely bring herself to look at him, let alone talk to him. Meals in the hall, attending chapel—even the simplest things became exercises in avoiding his gaze, complicated and full of potential embarrassment.

And she really shouldn't be trying to figure out whether he and Moll had been together, in any way, although so far, the answer seemed to be no. What Gavin did and with whom, as long as it didn't put their secret at risk or interfere with the training, wasn't important.

She could argue that getting intimate with Moll would endanger their secret and she could demand that he stay away from her, but then she would have to admit that she'd been paying attention.

Semeli, waiting beside her, leaned closer, drawing her back to the here and now. "Persians are the best doctors," she whispered out of the corner of her mouth. "Everybody knows that."

Fortunately, James was too busy studying her father to hear. "So you keep saying," Gwyneth pointed out in an even softer whisper as she absentmindedly patted Rufus's head. "Unfortunately, most Persian physicians are in Persia, not England."

James darted a condemning look at them. "And most Persian physicians don't speak our language. Now, if you don't mind, I prefer quiet."

Blushing furiously, Gwyneth nodded. She glanced at Semeli, who also looked suitably chastened.

Finally, James nodded and straightened, but he didn't immediately speak. He went to the basin and washed his hands before addressing her. "A word outside, my lady."

Gwyneth swallowed hard and tried not to be overly frightened. Maybe he was still angry with them for whispering. Maybe his brusque tone had nothing to do with her father's health.

"Semeli, straighten my father's bedding, please. And give him a drink of water if he wants one," she said as she went to the door. "Stay, Rufus."

Once on the stairway, James smiled and the expression in his gray eyes held good news. "I think you and your maidservant are right. He *is* getting stronger."

Gwyneth let out her breath in one great rush. "Thank the saints!" she cried softly as happiness overcame her dread. "And I'm sorry if our whispering disturbed you."

"I must confess it was a little distracting, but you are girls, and girls whisper. At least you didn't giggle. That I cannot abide."

"I was too afraid to find anything funny."

"Well, you may giggle a little after I am gone, for he is definitely improving," James answered with another kind smile. "I think your diligent care is responsible. Other men stronger than your father have died of such a fever."

The physician became grave. "However, I must tell you, he is not completely out of danger yet. He is still weak, and so at risk for another serious illness that could prove fatal. You must try to get him to eat more—good plain food to rebuild his strength. He should walk every day, too, at least around the chamber."

Gwyneth nodded and James put his hand on her shoulder. "You must take heart, my lady. The fact that he survived the first illness is nothing short of miraculous, so you must not give in to despair. However, you do need to know how important it is that he eat well and as much as he can, and walk as much as he can, too. I also think it would be wise not to worry him overmuch."

"I understand." Indeed, she had already been careful not to upset her father. She hadn't told him about the garrison's desertion, or DeVilliers's offer of protection. She had kept Thomas away from him and said nothing of the training of the men. As far as her father knew, everything was as it had been before he had gotten sick. "Is there any remedy you can give him to help speed his recovery?"

The physician shook his head. "I think not. God and nature, ably assisted by your devoted care, must do the rest."

"I thank you for all your help, James. Will you stay and sup with us?"

"Alas, no, my lady. I must get back to Salisbury as soon as possible. The bishop has fallen ill and needs my care." James shook his head. "There is so much conflict between the fortress garrison and the clergy at the cathedral, there is talk of building a new cathedral closer to the city. To my mind, it would be the best thing, but whatever happens, I fear the bishop's health will suffer until a decision is made. Now, if you will excuse me, my lady, I shall get my medicinal chest and depart at once. If I can, I will come again in a month's time to see how your father fares. Of course, should he fall seriously ill again, you must not hesitate to summon me."

"I will, and thank you, James." Gwyneth took the last remaining coins from the purse at her side and handed them to the physician. After he took them, she followed him back into her father's chamber. Tail wagging, Rufus came to greet her as if she'd been gone for days. Semeli, tidying the bed and nearby table, looked up, and when she saw Gwyneth's smile, smiled herself.

James took his chest and departed. Gwyneth sat on the stool beside her father, while Rufus laid his chin on the bed and regarded the earl as if he were the Holy Grail.

Her father gave Gwyneth a weary smile. "Well, little girl, it seems God is not ready for me yet."

"Not yet," she agreed, smiling, as pleased and relieved as if a great weight had fallen from her shoulders. It was one thing to hope he was getting better; it was another to have such a renowned physician say it.

"Where is Thomas? He has not tried to see me lately. I'm sure he must have plenty to complain about. He always does."

"He wanted to speak with you today," Gwyneth reluctantly confessed, "about the miller's weights again, but I thought James's visit would be tiring enough for you. I asked Thomas if it could wait. He said it could." She would not tell her father how grudgingly Thomas had agreed. "After all, nobody else thinks the miller is trying to cheat them with false weights. Now, you must not worry about the business of the estate, Father. It's in good hands."

For now, while Thomas still obeyed her and treated her with the respect due her birth.

She put such thoughts from her mind. "James says you are much better."

"Thanks to you, Gwyneth. Thanks to you. You will make some man an excellent wife."

She forced a genial smile onto her face. "I hope you are not in any hurry to be rid of me."

Her father chuckled. "Not at all, and frankly, I begin to fear that I may never think any man good enough for you, my daughter."

Certainly anyone less than a knight with a fine estate would not be "good enough," she was sure. A man who was not even a squire would stand no chance at all—which was completely unimportant and immaterial.

Her father sighed wearily as he patted Rufus. "James always tires me. I think I'll nap now."

"Yes, rest, Father."

"Send Peg to sit with me. But warn her that I have had enough of hearing about the time I fell into the river, and off my horse, and from the scaffold when the wall was being repaired. She likes to remind me of my past disasters, that woman."

Laughing softly, Gwyneth rose. It was true that Peg seemed to take some kind of fiendish delight regaling her father, and anyone who would listen, with reminiscences of his youthful accidents.

Gwyneth bent to kiss him gently on his broad forehead and brushed back a lock of white hair. "James says you are getting stronger, but you must eat more and try to walk around the chamber."

Lord William's eyes drifted closed. "More orders for the earl, eh?"

"Yes, more orders for the earl. Semeli, Rufus, and I will leave you now."

He didn't answer, and the gentle rising and falling of his chest told her he was already asleep.

The girls left the chamber and went down the stairs toward the hall, Rufus trotting off ahead of them.

"Was I not right?" Semeli demanded, her smile both happy and triumphant. "Did I not tell you he was getting better?"

"Yes, you did. I was just afraid to get my hopes up too much."

Semeli sniffed. "That is foolishness. He is getting well again, and Gavin is doing a better job than I ever thought he could. There is much to be happy about."

There was still much to be worried about, too, Gwyneth thought, and not just the baron.

She hadn't told Semeli about the kiss, as much as she wanted to. How could she? What would she say? That she had not acted like a lady? That she had enjoyed that kiss far too much? That she was always dreading Gavin would try to kiss her again, and then fearing that he wouldn't? That she was more confused and uncertain than ever, even though things were going better than she had dared to hope?

Worst of all, perhaps, even if her father recovered completely, things were never to be as they were, because she had met Gavin, the thief who could play the part of a squire so well. She found it easy to forget his low birth and dishonest past. He both looked and acted like a man nobly born, far more than she had ever guessed he could.

If only he really were a squire—or even better, a knight! Then she could hope . . . dream . . .

Such thoughts and dreams and hopes were no more than idle fantasies, and the sooner she drove them from her mind—and forgot about that kiss—the better off she would be. She must continue avoiding Gavin as best she could, too, if she could not control her wayward imagination.

If her heart protested, she would ignore it, too.

CHAPTER TEN

"You should go for a walk," Semeli suggested to Gwyneth a few days later as they sat mending beside the hearth in the hall. "You have been cooped up in the castle for too long."

"I appreciate your concern, but one near-meeting with thieves is quite enough," Gwyneth replied, her head bent over the gown she was mending.

"I did not mean the wood. It is a beautiful day. You could go to the river meadow and watch the men training." Semeli put her hand on Gwyneth's arm to get her to look up from her work.

"Do you not think you should encourage them with your presence?"

In her heart, Gwyneth knew Semeli was right. She should go and tell the men of Haverleigh she was pleased and proud, and that she appreciated their efforts. Just because Gavin would be there was no reason not to. Indeed, with so many people around, he wouldn't dare to be impertinent. "Very well, I shall. Will you come with me?" Gwyneth gave her friend a secretive, companionable smile. "After all, Hollis will be there."

Semeli tossed her head and raised her chin regally. "And what if he is?"

"You're right," Gwyneth replied with mock seriousness. "You'd probably distract him. Maybe you shouldn't go."

An equally knowing, mischievous look came to Semeli's brown eyes. "You might be distracted, too. It may take the two of us to make a proper judgment as to whether the men have learned all that Gavin of Inverlea can teach them."

Gwyneth's grin disappeared. "I don't know what you're talking about. How will I be distracted?"

"He takes his shirt off, you know."

Gwyneth immediately busied herself putting away her sewing and spoke without looking at Semeli. Leaning down also meant her face could be red from that effort, not a blush. "So what if he does? I've seen men half naked before."

"Farmers working in the fields, not handsome young squires," Semeli replied as she, too, put her mending in the basket at her feet. "And such muscles!" She slid Gwyneth another mischievous glance. "Why, even I am sometimes distracted, and *I* am a princess of Persia."

Gwyneth straightened and gave her a sour look. "Stop teasing. I don't care if he strips naked, and I've never noticed his muscles."

"You've gone blind, then?"

"Semeli," Gwyneth warned as she rose. She wasn't

enjoying her friend's teasing one bit, and she really didn't want to be forced to think about Gavin's physique.

"As you wish, my lady," Semeli replied with a wave of her hand. She, too, got to her feet. "You are above noticing such things. You pay no heed to his face, or his body, and I suppose you don't notice how the men respect him. And they like him, too."

Gwyneth paused as she reached down for her basket. "They do?"

"He has a gift for teaching," Semeli confirmed. "You could not have chosen better if you had searched the kingdom, I think."

Semeli was very serious, and her approval was not something easily given, to anyone. Gwyneth could also see that she wasn't just saying that because she wanted Gwyneth to accompany her. She really meant it.

"I'll find Peg and send her to sit with Father. She's probably in the kitchen. Will you take the mending to my chamber and meet me at the meadow?"

Semeli nodded her agreement and they parted.

As Gwyneth entered the kitchen, she saw Rufus nibbling on a bone. Herbs hung from the rafters, and two chickens roasted on an iron rod in the huge hearth, kept turning by the spit boy. Baskets of leeks and beans, plain fare rather than the richer foodstuffs other nobles would enjoy, were under the long, wooden work table. A lone scullery maid was busily scrubbing out the bread pans.

On another table, fresh loaves of plain brown bread sat cooling, the aroma filling the air. A large ginger cat strolled by, not a whit disturbed by Rufus's presence, for the cat ruled the kitchen, where he kept the mice at bay.

Etienne the cook looked up from the pot he was stirring and his round face broke into a smile. "Ah, my lady, how are you today?"

Gwyneth liked the plump fellow whose face always glistened with sweat because of the heat from the huge hearth.

She was also grateful he had stayed. A free man, he was his own master, and he was such a good cook, he could easily have found work with another noble family. Instead, out of loyalty to her father, he remained at Haverleigh. He made the most marvelous meals with the plainest of ingredients, something she appreciated more and more as they became poorer and poorer. "I'm looking for Peg. I've decided to go to the village and want her to sit with my father."

There was no need to tell Etienne she was going to the river meadow to watch the men train. Of course, there was no need to keep it a secret, either.

Etienne frowned and wiped his hands on his apron. His grave expression was so unusual, a shiver of dread skittered down her spine. "What is it, Etienne?"

"A word, if you please, my lady. In private." Etienne nodded at the buttery, where the large barrels of ale, called butts, were kept.

She followed him into the room, which contained only one barrel now. In days past, it would have been filled to the rafters. "Yes?"

"You saw those chickens roasting on the spit?"

"Yes."

"I am sorry to tell you this, my lady, but those are the last two chickens we have to eat. The other few we have left we should keep for eggs."

She slumped against the barrel. "James just told me my father needed good food." She thought a moment, then straightened. "We shall just have to find other meat."

"Your father cannot eat fish, or even eels. They upset his stomach," Etienne reminded her. "It is a pity your father did not purchase the right of free warren, for then we could have rabbits, pigeons—any of the lesser beasts we could catch in the wood."

Gwyneth frowned. "He didn't?"

"No, my lady. I asked him once, and he said he had not for the same reason he kept no hawks. He said he did not like to hunt."

That was certainly true. Her father had never enjoyed that sort of sport.

But that had been when they had more money and could purchase chickens, pigeons, pigs, and rabbits in addition to the stock that comprised part of the tenants' rent. They had finished the last pig four weeks ago, the pigeons sometime before that, and the last rabbit before Christmas.

She did not want to raise the rents when the last harvest had been so bad, but now, with the coffers empty and the last two chickens roasting on the spit, what else could she do? "Thank you for letting me know, Etienne."

As she left him to meet Semeli, she wracked her brain for another solution.

And then she found one.

In the dimmest corner of the tavern in Haverleigh where they were trying to be inconspicuous, Bert hunched over his mug of ale and frowned sourly at Fulk and Drogo. Smoke from the open hearth in the center of the room hung in the air, the small windows and thatched roof providing little ventilation. The walls were rough mud and dung plastered over woven sticks, and they had been blackened by the smoke. Rushes matted with spilled ale and wine covered the dirt floor, and scarred tables and benches comprised the furnishings.

"I don't understand why we even came back here," Bert whispered. "We shoulda gone on to Winchester—and we never should have gone to Aldenborough, neither. Soldiers everywhere, there was. We was lucky to get out alive."

Fulk scowled. "So DeVilliers likes to have a lot of

soldiers. We done all right, didn't we? Nobody caught us, did they? We're eatin', ain't we? So shut your gob and listen. That lad's body wasn't where we left it, and I want to know why."

"Animals," Drogo mumbled, already more than half in his cups. "Dragged it off and et it."

"Or he got up and walked away," Bert said. "Either way, he's gone, and there's the end to it. We don't need to risk our necks to find out. Let's just cut and run to Winchester."

"We could be riskin' our necks if we don't stay." Fulk spread his dirty, callused hands on the table and leaned toward them. "He knows about us, don't he?" he demanded in an impatient growl. "If he ain't dead, he can turn us in if he likes."

"He'd be puttin' his own neck in the noose if he did," Drogo pointed out, his words slurring. "'Sides, he ain't likely to be in Windus . . . Winjust . . . where we're headed, is he? He'd go t' London, maybe, or north to Edinburgh or York. He'll be wantin' to put some distance a-tween us, if he knows what's good fer 'im."

"Maybe, but I'd sleep better knowin' he was dead."

Fulk put his fingers to his lips, then half turned toward a group of peasants who were nearly finished with their midday repast of bread, cheese, and ale, the better to hear what they were saying.

"Gavin says we're starting with bows tomorrow," one

of the men said, a lanky farmer, by the look of him.

Fulk darted a sharp glance at his companions, then concentrated on the laborer, who was still speaking.

"I'm not keen on that, but it'll keep our Emlyn quiet. I only wish he'd give over all that wrestling."

"Especially when he keeps making you fight Darton, eh, Fenwick?" one of the others added with a chuckle.

"Well, you try getting a grip on him!" the one named Fenwick answered with a grin. "Like trying to get a stubborn ram in the fold. It's enough if I don't get bruised from collarbone to ankle."

"Aye, at least Emlyn will be pleased, anyway," added another fellow with dark hair. "I've never seen anybody sulk the way he does. Makes it almost an art. Gavin doesn't seem to mind that, though. He's a good sort, really, that Gavin. I think it was the hand of God brought him to Haverleigh."

Several of the men nodded their agreement.

"Wonder what Baron DeVilliers thinks?" the dark-haired man mused. "He's been waitin' like a vulture coming to pick over Haverleigh. That won't be so easy now, eh?"

The men exchanged more grins and chuckles.

"Neighbor or not," Fenwick said, "he's a right greedy bastard. I no more want him lord of Haverleigh than I would want Satan himself for a master."

"Aye," several muttered in agreement.

"And I tell ya, I get right sick thinking of him marrying our sweet Lady Gwyneth. Like her sainted mother, she is, and I'd rather see her in a convent than wed to one like DeVilliers."

"Pity Gavin's a Scot," another, skinny fellow said. "Otherwise, I'd be putting a wager on that match."

"Scot?" Drogo muttered, his eyes half closed.

Fulk silenced him with a hiss.

"You think a man in the service of Sir Henry D'Argent isn't a good match, Scot or no?" Fenwick protested. "A pity he's so young, more like. Still, I wouldn't say there's no hope there. He's a handsome lad, and she's a comely lass. He's a squire, she's a lady."

"It'll be the earl what decides in the end who his daughter will marry," the dark-haired man pointed out.

"Aye. Now we'd best be gettin' to the meadow," the skinny fellow said as he hauled himself to his feet. "Gavin'll be waitin' and the last time I was late, he made me run to the river and back four times. Thought I was going to die of thirst, I did."

"It was a thirst for ale what made you late, and he knew it," Fenwick replied with a chortle. "The earl would 'ave put you in the stocks if you'd come to do your service in such a state as that. I tell ya, he's a good sort, our Gavin."

As the other peasants nodded their agreement and filed out of the tavern, Fulk turned to his companions and raised one eyebrow.

"Did you hear that, you nits?" he hissed. "*Our* Gavin. Dead, eh? Dragged off by animals, eh? Neck in a noose, eh? Seems the hand of God moves in mysterious ways. *Our Gavin's* landed on his feet, and these fools don't have the first notion who or what he is."

"Maybe it's somebody else," Drogo suggested. "Sounds like a soldier doing some training. That can't be *our* Gavin. He's just a lad. And he's not a Scot."

"Maybe it's somebody else," Fulk repeated in a mocking whisper. "What are you, touched in the head? How many Gavins can there be? He's taller than you, and smarter. And his whore of a mother was a Scot. Maybe he's told 'em he was a soldier and they believed him."

"I've met plenty of Berts in my day," Bert noted helpfully.

Fulk raised his hand to hit him, then stopped himself after a swift glance around the tavern showed the plump serving wench clearing away the mugs left on the other tables. "Whoever this Gavin is, we ain't leavin' here until we've seen 'im, and that's final."

"What if it *is* our Gavin and he's fooled them into thinking he's a soldier?"

Fulk regarded Drogo steadily. "Then he's a dead soldier.

But not for a while. I'm thinkin' this Baron DeVilliers might want to know what's goin' on here. That kind of information should be worth a pretty penny. But first we'll have to find out if that's *our* Gavin, one way or another."

CHAPTER ELEVEN

The men sat in the meadow in a large circle, their swords at their sides as Gavin and Hollis faced each other. Gavin liked to finish every day with another lesson in hand-to-hand fighting. He believed with all his heart that could make the difference between life and death if these men ever had to fight in a pitched battle.

"Hollis, you're getting better, but you've got to keep your hands *up*. Now, bob . . . weave . . . keep your eyes on me. Now, advance." He backed up as Hollis, right foot forward, moved toward him.

"You've got to protect your jaw, your nose, and especially your eyes," he continued. "A blow on your jaw can shatter it, or your teeth. Somebody's fist to your nose can break it and send the bone back into your head, killing you at once." He pointed to the bone above his brow. "Although it might not kill you, you can bleed a lot if you're hit here. If the blood flows, you'll be blinded, and an easy target."

"This wrestling is all very well if you're a foot soldier," Emlyn muttered loud enough for Gavin to hear. "It won't do archers any good."

"Provided the enemy doesn't break through the line and attack you," Gavin noted.

He pretended he was going to hit Hollis's chin. As he jabbed, Hollis's fist hooked around and smacked Gavin's arm away.

Hard.

"That hurt!" Gavin cried.

Looking very pleased with himself, Hollis straightened. "I was keeping my eyes on you, just like you said, and hit fast like a snake striking, just like you said."

The men chuckled, until Gavin shoved Hollis to the ground with his shoulder and raised his foot as if about to kick him in the head. "Got you again, Hollis. You really have to keep your guard up."

Grinning, Hollis held out his hand. "Help me up, and I'll have another go."

"I think you look like fleas jumping around on a dog's back," Semeli announced from somewhere close by.

Gavin turned and found her standing near Emlyn, smiling as if she were vastly amused.

"So what if they do?" he demanded, wondering if she would have said that if Lady Gwyneth were with her. "Nobody will be able to land a punch then."

"I could."

"Really?"

Her smile grew. "Of course. I am a princess of Persia."

"I didn't know Persian princesses were famous for their fighting skills."

Instead of looking annoyed at his gibe, Semeli continued to smile serenely. "Obviously you know nothing at all about Persian princesses."

"Perhaps you'd care to show us?" Gavin replied dryly, expecting that to silence her. Then he would tell her to go back to the castle, where she belonged.

"As you wish, I shall demonstrate."

As Gavin watched, stunned and not sure what to say, she rolled up her sleeves, revealing the hard curve of muscle.

She did look very strong—for a girl—and she sounded so calm and sure of herself, Gavin wished he had kept quiet. Then he noticed Hollis, grinning like a fool. "Hollis!"

The lad started. "Eh?"

"You may show Semeli what you've learned."

"With pleasure!"

Gavin didn't think Hollis should sound quite so delighted by the prospect of being knocked down by a girl, even if that was highly unlikely.

They went to the center of the circle. Hollis crouched and held his fists in front of his chin, just as Gavin had shown him. He swayed from side to side on the balls of his feet.

Semeli just stood there and waited.

Maybe he should put a stop to this. He didn't want to see a girl get hurt.

Then, as Hollis continued to dance around, Semeli slowly leaned a little forward and held her arms wide, as if inviting him to hug her.

"I don't want to hit you, Semeli," Hollis warned, panting a little, "but I will if I can."

"Go ahead. Try."

"All right."

There was more swaying, more dancing on his toes. Semeli watched and waited. Then Hollis moved his hand out to strike. In one swift motion, she grabbed it, twisted it behind his back, and got her other arm around his throat.

"No man should ever try to hit a princess of Persia," she said, barely winded.

"How did you do that?" Gavin asked eagerly, too impressed by the move to be concerned about Hollis's possible embarrassment. "Can you show us?"

Semeli let go, and Hollis rubbed his neck. Instead of looking upset, however, Hollis regarded Semeli with blatant admiration. "Yes, show us."

She shook her head. "Not today. I have work to do."

"Soon?"

"Soon," she agreed with a nod.

Then Gavin spotted Lady Gwyneth coming down the road, Rufus trotting along beside her. He should be pleased for the men's sake, he supposed, and if she was coming to check on his instruction and was happy with the results, he could leave.

Which was what he wanted, of course, despite the comforts he was enjoying here, for he was still subject to Lady Gwyneth's commands, and the risk of imprisonment, or worse. He should be keen to shake the dust of Haverleigh from his feet.

Yet as the girl who held his fate in his hands drew near, he knew he didn't want to leave Haverleigh. He would miss the men and their friendship as much as the respect they gave him. He would miss having his own place to sleep, and decent clothes to wear. He would miss feeling safe and secure. He would even miss Lady Gwyneth, despite her cool and distant manner, for she was the first person who had ever given him a chance to be something other than a thief.

"Get up, everybody," he ordered as he drew on his shirt. "The lady of Haverleigh is coming."

With pleased murmurs, they stood and waited for her to join them. Meanwhile, Gavin put a smile on his face, for their sake.

As Lady Gwyneth joined him in the center of the circle and Rufus settled on his haunches beside her, Gavin realized she looked as worried as she had that first day when she proposed her plan. What more had happened to upset her? Was it her father's illness, or the baron, or something else entirely?

In spite of the concern that lingered in her eyes, she smiled at the men. "I have heard how well you all are doing," she announced. "I want you all to know how pleased I am."

A delighted murmur went up from the men, and they exchanged proud smiles.

"Would you like them to show you what they've learned?" Gavin asked, telling himself this was a reasonable question and had nothing to do with getting her attention.

She gave him the briefest and coolest of glances. "If they're not too tired."

"Not a bit!" Hollis cried. "Are we?"

Some of the older men looked as if they wanted to say they were. Nevertheless, all nodded their assent.

"Right," Gavin said briskly, keeping his gaze on them and not on Lady Gwyneth. "Pair off and we'll start with the sword drills."

They began practicing the moves as he had shown them. For now, they were careful not to hurt their opponent, yet he was sure that if they had to fight, they would instinctively react with more force and a lot less care. Their bodies had learned the feel of the swing, the quick response to block another's blow, the waiting stance.

As he watched them and surreptitiously noted Lady Gwyneth's pleased and even awed expression, a pride such as he had never felt before blossomed within him. *He* had done this; he was responsible. He had not failed.

Would she acknowledge that, or would she simply accept it as the job she expected him to do?

"Enough," he called out. "Put down your swords. Change partners with the man to your right. Hollis, you will be with Darton. Now we will show your lady your hand-to-hand skills."

Hollis approached the bare knuckle champion of three shires with a weary acceptance.

"Darton will hurt Hollis," Lady Gwyneth murmured in protest.

"Don't be so sure. Hollis is my best student," Gavin confessed, something he hadn't even told Hollis.

In truth, he could knock him down only by trickery, and Semeli had defeated Hollis, Gavin believed, because he had let her. Man to man, Hollis was faster, tougher, and despite his appearance, stronger than most.

His theory was soon proven, for with one quick feint, turn, and shove, Darton was flat on his back. Gwyneth and Semeli clapped their approval, while Rufus started to bark.

"That was a wonderful trick!" Lady Gwyneth cried.

She faced Gavin, her eyes aglow with pleasure and her cheeks pink with excitement. "Oh, I knew you could do it! I'd wager they could defeat even the king's army now!"

"I did my best."

As Gavin looked at the young lady who had made him a squire, if only a false one, something beyond pride or even happiness bloomed in his heart, something composed of hope and yearning. Maybe she *could* overlook his past of poverty and theft. Maybe she could see in him the potential to be a better man, one with a future. Perhaps she would even invite him to stay on a while longer.

Gwyneth looked away, and the pink tinge on her cheeks deepened to a blush. "Yes, well, you've done wonders, considering."

Considering?

All the joy he had felt only moments before died and became like the ashes of a fire that had burned out long ago. He might be able to forget who and what he was, but she never would.

By the saints, he was no better than a moonstruck dolt concocting fantastic tales of an impossible future that paid no heed to rank or wealth. He must have been temporarily mad to think she would ask him to stay, and even more to kiss her.

"Was that not what I was told to do, my lady, on pain of death?" he inquired in a harsh whisper that only she could hear.

Her gaze faltered.

He didn't care if she was distressed. Why should he? He was just her lackey, after all.

"Enough," Gavin called again, and the men stopped wrestling to regard her expectantly.

"I am *very* pleased," she reiterated, her cheeks still pink as she moved away from him to address the men. "You have all done better than I had dared to hope. If we are attacked, we shall be a force to be reckoned with. I only wish I were a man so that I could have been here learning with you. Yet know you this, men of Haverleigh—if it comes to a battle, I will be on the battlements doing what I can."

"Aye, with your bow, eh?" Emlyn called out.

The men all laughed and nodded.

Gavin turned to her with a cold glare. "Is this another thing you should have told me—that you know how to shoot a bow?"

She flushed, and he was glad to see her discomfort. It was but a small repayment for the way she made him feel. "Yes. Emlyn's father taught me."

"I tell you, she's better than me, and that's saying something," Emlyn called out, both complimenting Gwyneth and boasting at the same time.

Gavin turned his lips up into a sardonic little smile, not caring if he made her angry or not. What did it matter, anyway? He was going to be leaving here as soon as he possibly could, whether she gave him permission or not. "You are full of surprising talents, my lady."

Her blush deepened, and his fiendish delight increased.

Ignoring him, she again addressed the men. "You have my leave to go and again, I thank you."

The men gave her a bow, and then began to gather up their things. As they did, Gavin turned to march back to the castle, until she put her hand on his arm to hold him back. "I need to talk to you, Gavin. In my father's solar, his private room where business is usually conducted——"

"I know what a solar is, my lady," he snapped, fighting not to let her touch affect him.

As for the private business she wanted to discuss, he wouldn't be surprised to hear it was time for him to go, and there would be dire consequences if he ever revealed their secret.

Determined to get the meeting over and done with, he held out his arm to escort her. She slipped hers through, just as she had other times.

As they walked, he commanded himself to ignore her. He must ignore her. After all, soon he would be far away from here. And her. And everything that would recall his foolish, hopeful, yet ultimately hopeless delusion.

They left the field and continued on in stony silence to the castle, then across the courtyard. Rufus left them there and headed to the kitchen, so they were alone when they reached the solar, a round room in the south tower. It was warm from the sun, and bare of all furnishings, an unexpected reminder that she was not as rich as she seemed.

Gavin stood stiff and tense, as if he were a prisoner awaiting judgment. "Well, are you going to tell me to go?" he demanded without waiting for her to begin. "We haven't started with the bows yet, but apparently *you* can teach them that."

She turned to face him, and to his shock, he saw genuine surprise and confusion cloud her pretty face. "No, I did not ask you here to tell you to leave."

His eyes narrowed with suspicion, too wary to get his hopes up again, lest they be dashed once more. "Then why?"

"I have had some disturbing news. My father is doing better, but he must have good food to make him strong. Unfortunately, we have no more animals to slaughter, and he cannot eat fish or eels. They made him sick even when he was in the prime of his health."

That was all? He could stay . . . if he wanted to. She drew in a ragged breath, and the sound struck at the wall of his wounded pride and fierce self preservation, and he thought of what she had said. They had no meat, and her ailing father required it.

He had forgotten that she was just a girl trying to do the best she could for her family and the people who relied on her. "Is there nothing left to sell to purchase what you need?"

"A few more bits of furniture that will buy only enough for a day or two for the household. The weapons, which we may need. There are my brother's armor and other things from when he was a knight, but selling them must be the very last resort."

"Have you not come to the last resort?" he asked gently.

"I was thinking that perhaps you could . . ." Her hands clasped, she fell silent, a blush upon her cheeks.

Understanding burst upon him. "That I could *steal* some meat for you?"

He bit back a curse and silenced the cry of dismay wrung from his heart at this new and forceful reminder of what he was to her, and what he would ever be. "After all," he said coldly, "I am a thief. Who do you suggest I steal from?" he asked, raising an inquiring brow. "Your beloved tenants?"

"There are rabbits and deer in the wood."

"Then why don't you ask some of your tenants to hunt for you?"

"My father was not a keen hunter, so he saw no reason to pay for the right of free warren. By law, therefore, all the game in our wood belongs to the king."

"So you're asking me to be a poacher." He sidled closer to her, running a scornful gaze over her. "Do you not know the penalty for poaching?"

She did not look away. She met his purposefully insolent gaze steadily. Boldly. Bravely. "You have already broken the law many times, I think."

He took hold of her by the shoulders and brought his face close to hers, so that he was looking directly into her brilliant blue eyes. "So what is it to me to risk my life, or have my fingers cut off or my eyes put out—is that it?"

She twisted away and he let her go. "I know maiming is the penalty for poaching, but I want my father to live, and for that, he needs meat! I am desperate, Gavin, and I thought you could help me." She marched to the door. "Forget that I asked you. I should not have suggested you take that risk. I'll sell all that I can, even my brother's things."

She put her hand on the latch, ready to leave.

If she left him now, like this, he would always be the thief who had refused to help her father.

He crossed the room in two long strides and covered her hand with his.

She looked up at him. God save him, she had beautiful eyes.

His rage dissipated like smoke in the wind. "To be a poacher, you have to be able to hunt," he admitted quietly. "I can't. I've never had the weapons, for you don't hunt with a broadsword. Besides, I made my living stealing, not hunting. I can defend myself against armed men, or steal chickens and wring their necks, but I have never hunted an animal in a wood in my life."

As disappointment replaced her ire, he moved away, putting some distance between them, then faced her again. "You would probably be a better hunter than me, if you really are skilled with a bow."

"Oh."

He approached her slowly, warily. "But I will help you as best I can, my lady. Don't sell anything else. I suspect that unlike some, Emlyn's skill with a bow has not been used solely to hit practice targets. Let me find out, and if so, I will persuade him to take me hunting."

Hope flared in her lovely eyes and her parted lips seemed to draw him like a moth to a flame—until she frowned.

"Even if what you think is true," she said, "Emlyn won't confess he's done something dishonest to a squire."

"Do you think no squires hunt where they should not? I have met a few poachers in my travels, and to hear them tell it, half of the game they were blamed for killing was really taken by young noblemen who hunt for sport. The fact that it's against the law adds to the excitement for them. I will put it to Emlyn in such a way that he will think I am one of them."

"If he agrees, you should not go with him if you cannot hunt."

"I am not a coward. And I want to help. Being with a squire, even a false one, should protect Emlyn if we are seen or caught by the reeve or any of the villagers. Thomas would surely think twice about arresting me, and anybody with me."

She raised her glowing eyes shining with gratitude and respect, and his heart seemed to twist as if it was never going to be the same again. "You may be right."

He moved as close as he dared. "You know I am."

"Very well, but you must tell me when you plan to hunt. I can send Thomas off the estate on an errand to Salisbury, so there will be one less thing for you to be concerned about."

Gavin nodded and smiled. She smiled in return.

The air seemed to thicken around them, as if creating a place where they were apart from anything and everyone, where they were just a boy and a girl, not a thief and a lady. Where the mistakes he had made seemed to dwindle to unimportance, and apology seemed an easy thing to do. "I'm sorry I kissed you and I ask your forgiveness."

Gwyneth's hand went to her lips, as if he had done it only moments ago. "Of course I forgive you."

Then she put her arms around him and brought her mouth to his.

CHAPTER TWELVE

As Gwyneth stopped kissing him and stepped away, Gavin stared at her with disbelief as much as pleasure. "I thought you didn't want me to kiss you again."

"You didn't. This time, *I* kissed *you*." Gwyneth warmed with embarrassment, but she wasn't sorry she had done it.

When he had faced her, offering to help again despite the greater risk she was asking him to take, her heart had seemed to flutter at his soft words, and a feeling she had never felt before blossomed within her. It was not the same as the excitement she had felt in the armory. This was deeper, like a movement in the depths of her being. It made her feel young and older simultaneously, and as if something was changing and would never be the same, the way the illness of her father had altered her world—but in a much better way. It was as if she were leaving childhood behind for something . . . more.

"Why did you do it?" Gavin asked, confused and more uncertain than she had ever seen him, even when he'd faced the men that first day.

Why, indeed? How could she put her feelings into words? "Because . . . because I'm grateful for your help, for everything you've done," she said, turning away. "You should go now. If we are alone together for too long, people will talk."

He came up behind her, and when he spoke, his voice was a low, husky whisper that made her pulse pound. "What will they say?"

"That you and I . . . that we . . ."

Frustrated by his questions, dismayed and excited by his closeness, she turned and faced him. That was a mistake, for he was inches away from her.

In spite of that, she forced herself to speak. "I'm sure you can guess what they'll say."

"Yes, I can." He didn't look angry or upset. He looked resigned, and she told herself that was good. He was a thief, she was a lady, and they could not—must not—forget that, no matter how they felt.

"I will speak to Emlyn tomorrow," he said. "We start with the bows, which should please him no end, so he'll probably be in a good humor and agree to take me hunting."

"Gavin, I am truly grateful for all your help, despite my threats. You are so clever, I'm sure you could have gotten away plenty of times if you'd wanted to. I'm very glad you didn't."

He reached out and took her hands in his strong, warm ones and she could scarcely breathe.

"Perhaps it pleased me to have a pretty lady in need of

my help," he said softly. "Perhaps I liked playing the squire, if only for a little while."

She swallowed hard as she looked up into his intense brown eyes that seemed to be asking a question of her.

No matter what she wanted, what her heart demanded, he simply could not stay at Haverleigh. As much as she hoped it could be otherwise, he could not pretend to be a squire forever. Sooner or later the baron was going to come, and if he didn't guess the truth, he would surely do all in his power to learn what he could of Sir Henry D'Argent's squire. When that happened, Gavin had to be gone.

As for what would happen to her if the baron learned the truth . . . this ruse would be the ammunition he needed to force her to marry him, either on pain of exposing her if he realized she was willingly involved, or as proof that she was utterly incapable of ruling Haverleigh if he thought she had been tricked.

She slowly, reluctantly, pulled her hands from Gavin's. "For whatever reason," she said, trying to give her words a serenity she certainly didn't feel, "you have my thanks, and you will have my father's, too, when he knows of it."

Disappointment, swift and deep, flashed in Gavin's eyes, yet he merely nodded and went to the door.

"Good day, my lady," he said with a bow as he reached for the latch.

"Good day," she answered as she watched him leave.

Then she walked to the window and looked out over

the courtyard and the walls of the castle, beyond the village to the wood where she had first seen Gavin.

Despite everything that had gone before, never had her home seemed such a prison, or the obligations of her rank so terrible.

The next day it took only a little while for Gavin to see that Emlyn was indeed very good with a bow. He hit the bull's-eye in the targets spread over the mounds of hay at the far end of the river meadow nearly every time.

Gavin walked along the row of men lined up about a hundred feet away from the targets. Nearby stood a work-horse of great age hitched to a cart that had carried the bows and arrows, butts of hay, and targets to the meadow.

Although Gavin was watching, he wasn't really paying much heed to what they were doing, leaving it to Emlyn to give instruction, correction, and the order to let loose.

He had other things to think about, like asking Emlyn to go poaching with him, and Lady Gwyneth's kiss.

He had never been more pleased and confused in his life than when she did that, but why had she? Because she was simply grateful, as she'd said? Because she didn't under-stand how much that kiss had seemed to promise?

She must have no idea at all of the hopes she had inspired in him, which were greater now than they had ever been. He had scarcely dared to conceive of a future here at

Haverleigh, let alone one with her, but that kiss suggested that she felt more than mere gratitude for a job well done.

He *must* be exaggerating its significance. She was a lady; he was a thief. She was noble; he most certainly was not. She was young and naïve about the world; he was probably going to wind up swinging from a rope at a crossroads, his body left hanging there as a warning to others who would steal.

If he were wise, he would destroy any ridiculous hopes he harbored before they grew even stronger. If he were really wise, he thought grimly, he would leave Haverleigh at once.

"Release!" Emlyn shouted, and suddenly a volley of arrows flew through the air. Some hit the targets, more stuck in the ground in front of them, and a few landed on the ground beside them.

As Gavin absently watched the men retrieve the arrows, something moved in the willow trees near the river.

He stiffened and stared, trying to see what it was. He didn't see any sign of people walking there, or trying to hide, either, yet something had definitely been moving through the trees.

Had DeVilliers learned what he was doing and sent men to see? Had he been wrong to think Fulk and the others would leave the area without making sure he was dead?

He ran his hand through his hair. The longer he stayed here, the more dangerous it was. He had trained the men the best he could. There was nothing more to keep him here . . . except Gwyneth, and the offer to go hunting.

When he saw no other signs of movement, he told himself Fulk and the others were surely far away, or he would have seen signs of their presence before this. DeVilliers had not ventured from his castle or his own estate of Aldenborough, or so the men claimed. Nobody looked at him as if they suspected he was anything other than what he claimed to be. Just to be sure, though, he would check the riverbank when the practice was over.

"God save me, I'm not doing this another time!" Hollis exclaimed.

He threw down his bow in disgust and rubbed his left forearm as he glared at Emlyn, who bustled over as if he'd been personally insulted.

Gavin also hurried toward the obviously angry Hollis. The other men gathered around.

"What happened?" Gavin asked as he halted beside Hollis.

"The bloody bowstring," Hollis cried. "Look at my arm!"

He thrust his left arm out. It was already bruising.

Emlyn shrugged. "You're not holding the bow right, is all." He turned to Gavin. "The bowstring slapped his forearm when he let loose. Hurts like hell, I grant you, but it's not worth such a fuss."

"I *was* holding the bloody bow right—or at least the way you said. I thought we were supposed to defend ourselves with those things, not be wounded. My arm'll be black and blue for a week!"

"Well, if you can't do it right—" Emlyn retorted.

"I'm not the only one." Hollis gestured to the men in a circle around them. "Look."

They all put out their forearms, and an array of bruises appeared.

"Aye, maybe we'd better forget this archery nonsense," Fenwick grumbled. "Our arms are going to fall off before we're any good."

"Telling you I am, you've just got to hold it right," Emlyn insisted. He picked up his bow and pulled an arrow from the quiver at his side. He nocked it, slipping the groove at the feathered end of the arrow into the bowstring. He lifted the bow and pulled back on the string with the three fingers of his right hand, then released it. The arrow sliced through the air to land in the center of the nearest target. He lowered the bow. "See? Not hard at all."

Gavin nodded at the leather strip laced on Emlyn's left forearm. "I notice you've got a guard."

"Well, yes. But I don't need it."

"Then why wear it?" Hollis demanded.

"Why don't you try a bow and see for yourself, Gavin?" Darton suggested.

Thinking this would end the conflict quickly, Gavin agreed. "All right, I will."

Emlyn looked as if he'd been given a prize. "It's not hard at all, with a little practice. Give us some room there, the rest of you, if you please."

The others spread out, leaving a large space between Emlyn and Gavin, and a clear view of one of the targets. "Now then, your left side to the target."

Apparently Emlyn was under the impression he had learned nothing by observing. Or else he was just so excited to be giving archery lessons, he wanted to start again at the beginning.

"I know that much from listening and watching you," Gavin remarked.

"Yes, well, of course," Emlyn replied, flushing slightly. "Now, bow in the left hand and fit the nock of the arrow into the string with your right. That's it. Hold the arrow in place with the first three fingers of your right. Lift the bow and draw the string back to your chin. Some pull all the way back to the ear, but the chin will do for now. Hold the bow straight."

That proved more difficult than Gavin had suspected, just as the bowstring offered more resistance than he had imagined. A man needed strong arms to be a bowman, which made him wonder how strong Gwyneth was. Perhaps she had muscles like Semeli. He would likely never know.

"Better, better. Now, take your aim along the shaft

of the arrow. Some look above the tip, but I don't agree. The shaft is better."

Gavin did as he was told.

"Release!"

Gavin did.

And instantly cried out the most colorful curse he knew. The string had snapped against his left arm like a leather strap in the hands of a strong man. It stung and burned, all at the same time.

He gulped for breath and silently cursed himself again, this time for letting that word slip. A squire probably wouldn't use such language.

A quick glance at the men, however, showed that they were sympathetic rather than shocked.

"You see?" Hollis declared, justified, as Gavin held his sore arm. "He was holding it right, wasn't he, Emlyn?"

"Pretty good, but not perfect, or it wouldn't have hurt," the Welshman insisted.

Trying not to show that his skin still burned, Gavin pressed his lips together as the men started to argue.

"He was—as perfect as you, at any rate," Hollis declared.

"You've got that arm guard—that makes all the difference," Fenwick noted.

"Yes, I want an arm guard, too," Darton said, "or I ain't doing this no more."

"Bows are for Welshman, anyway, not Saxons," Hollis

muttered. "Give me a sword any day, or an ax."

Gavin held up his hand to silence them. "How long does it take to get good enough for that not to happen?" he asked Emlyn.

The little Welshman shrugged. "Depends on the bowman."

There was more angry muttering from the men.

"Unless we can all have guards," Gavin said, still clutching his arm, "we'd be better off hurling rocks and spears from the walls than trying to shoot arrows."

"But —!"

"Emlyn, you may be an excellent archer," Gavin interrupted, trying to be as diplomatic as he could, "and I'm sure the earl will allow anybody else who can figure out how to use a bow without hurting himself to be an archer, but for now, I think the rest of us will do better with swords. Let's call it a day, shall we?"

A murmur of approval ran through the men.

"Unstring your bows and load them in the cart. You three, take down the targets. Emlyn, I would like to talk with you a moment."

The men eagerly agreed and did as they were told, muttering among themselves. Emlyn, meanwhile, looked as if he'd lost his best friend.

"I'll walk with you to retrieve the arrows that went far to the right," Gavin offered.

Emlyn sullenly nodded his agreement and they

started toward the river.

"I'll be sure to tell Lord William of your skill," Gavin began.

Emlyn tilted his head and looked up at Gavin morosely. "He already knows."

Gavin decided to forget trying to cheer Emlyn up. "I think I saw something moving down by the river. Maybe one of the arrows hit an animal. Perhaps it's only wounded. We should check that, too."

They passed the targets and walked along the river bank, but an army could have marched through, the ground was so churned up.

"They bring the livestock here to drink in the morning," Emlyn explained when he saw Gavin's expression, and he seemed a little less upset. "And I'm not seeing any blood."

"No, neither am I," Gavin replied. He would find no answers here, and he hoped that he had been wrong.

He halted and bent to pull another arrow out of the mud. "Tell me, do you only ever shoot at bull's eyes painted on a sheet?" he asked matter-of-factly.

Emlyn slid Gavin a cautious glance as Gavin handed him the arrow. He put it in the quiver hanging from his belt. "Sometimes I pick other targets. A tree limb, that sort of thing."

They began walking back toward the village. As they went, Emlyn and Gavin gathered fallen arrows as if they were harvesting them from the field.

"I'd like to see you really put your skill to the test," Gavin remarked.

"What, with a contest or some such?"

"Not exactly. You see, Emlyn, the other excellent archers I've known have always told me that the true test of skill is a moving target."

"Did they?"

"Yes, they did. Once or twice they've let me come along while they did the testing."

"Been on some hunts, then, have you?"

"Yes." Gavin straightened and looked around to make sure nobody could hear them, noting as he did that Semeli had joined Hollis at the cart.

Semeli didn't look happy.

Well, that was none of his concern. He had enough to think about without troubling himself about Hollis's relationship with a girl. "The other excellent archers I've known didn't set any store in forest law, either, if you follow me, Emlyn."

Emlyn gasped as if shocked, but his eyes were far too shrewd. "They were poachers?"

"I suppose poaching would have been the charge, if they had ever been caught."

The Welshman toyed with the feathers on the end of the arrow Gavin had just handed him. "That's against the law. There's heavy penalties for poaching. I could lose my fingers, or an eye."

"*If* you got caught. Of course, *I* would be with you. And I suppose there's no harm in telling you, Lord William is in serious need of good food. Some venison or rabbit stew would be most welcome."

Emlyn continued to finger the feathers. He wet his lips. "Seems a bit of a risky way for a fellow to prove his skill."

Emlyn was right and Gavin wouldn't deny it. "Yes, I suppose it is."

"I don't know the woods as well as Hollis, neither."

"Ah."

"If he could come, that'd be . . . different."

"Really?"

"Aye."

"Do you think he would?"

Emlyn grinned, and his eyes danced with sly mischief. "Aye. Likes prowling about the woods, Hollis does."

CHAPTER THIRTEEN

Gavin left Emlyn to finish collecting the stray arrows and hurried to talk to Hollis. He halted a few feet away as Semeli turned and marched off. He thought—incredible though it seemed, given her usual air of majestic serenity—that she was crying.

"Hollis, can you spare me a moment?" he asked his friend, wondering whether he should inquire about what had happened, or mind his own business.

Hollis faced him, the usual grin on his face. However, the youth's eyes looked more miserable than Gavin would ever have believed possible. "As a matter o' fact, I was goin' to ask if you'd care t' join me for a bite at the tavern."

That seemed rather a public place for what he wanted to ask, Gavin thought. On the other hand, it would probably be crowded with men talking, and sometimes it was just as easy to have a private conversation in a crowded room as anywhere else.

Besides, as he regarded Hollis's sad eyes, he didn't want to deny this simple request. "I'd be happy to," he replied, and together they headed for the tavern.

"That's good news about Lord William gettin' better,"

Hollis offered as they walked.

"Yes, it is. And that's what I wanted to talk to you about."

Hollis stopped. "It's true, ain't it? Semeli says so."

"I never doubted it was," Gavin answered honestly.

They walked along in silence for a while. Gavin told himself he shouldn't worry about what he had just witnessed between Hollis and Semeli. It was none of his concern. Hollis wasn't his man, or in his employ. He was just a . . . friend.

Weren't friends supposed to help each other? Or should he also ignore the troubles of the first friend he had ever really had?

He didn't want to ignore Hollis, or his troubles, any more than he wanted to ignore Gwyneth.

Still, this was all new to him, and he felt awkward and unsure where to begin. "Hollis, I couldn't help noticing that you and Semeli . . . that is, she looked a little upset."

"Aye, she is. I'm leaving Haverleigh, and she doesn't want me to go." He glanced sharply at Gavin, as if he expected him to protest. "I'm not bonded to Haverleigh. I can go if I want."

Gavin was shocked, but not for that reason. "You're leaving? Why?"

Hollis shrugged and walked on. "Lots o' reasons."

"If you don't want to tell me, I'll understand," Gavin

said as he caught up to him. "It's none of my business."

Hollis sighed. "There's no reason you shouldn't know. But my throat's as dry as an old bone, so once we've got a mug in our hands, I'll tell you—and you should tell me what you wanted to talk to me about. It's more important, I'm sure."

"It's important, but it can wait a bit."

The tavern they entered was like lots of other taverns Gavin had been in, the air smoky and heavy with the scent of wet rushes and stale ale. The furniture was simple— wooden benches and tables, not new, but Gavin had seen plenty worse.

Several of the men who had been in the meadow were there, laughing and talking. They greeted Gavin and Hollis with friendly hails, and a few jested about Gavin having come down in the world if he was keeping Hollis company. He laughed as required, but in his heart he knew that if he could truly count Hollis as a friend, he had come up in the world.

Once Gavin and Hollis were seated, the others mercifully went back to their own conversations.

A plump middle-aged woman with messy brown hair and very few teeth came toward them. She surveyed them from head to toe. "Well, my handsome young squire that I've been hearin' so much about and my homely young scalawag, what'll you have?"

Apparently Hollis took no offense at being called

homely or a scalawag. "I'm standing the squire an ale," he announced as if he did this sort of thing all the time. "And one of your fine meat pies, Sally."

"For which this squire will be very grateful," Gavin added.

"Come into some money lately, have you, me lad?" Sally replied, raising her brows questioningly.

"I have enough," Hollis replied. He reached into his tunic and pulled out a threadbare purse. He opened it and retrieved a silver coin. "See?"

Sally nodded. "Right you are, then!"

Gavin tried not to look or feel embarrassed, but he knew that was a lot of money for Hollis. "I mean it, Hollis, I'm very grateful. Those thieves took all my money, or I would gladly—"

"'Ere now, shut your gob!" Hollis exclaimed. Then he frowned and blushed bright red. "I mean to say, Gavin, never you mind. It's my pleasure."

Hollis would have his pride, too, so Gavin decided he would say no more about the cost. "Now, why are you leaving Haverleigh?" he asked his red-haired friend.

Gavin was surprised to see the depth of anger that came to Hollis's usually merry eyes. "My stepfather. He's never liked me, and he doesn't like Semeli, either. He says I shouldn't even talk to her because she's beneath me. I am freeborn, and she was a slave."

"Plenty of people would agree with Thomas about you

being friends with Semeli," Gavin reluctantly admitted.

"Do *you?*" he demanded, bristling still more, and Gavin suddenly realized that beneath that genial exterior lurked a man with the makings of a fierce warrior.

"No, I don't," he answered honestly. "I know enough to judge a person by how they treat others, not their rank."

The gleam returned to Hollis's eyes as he nodded. "I thought so, because of the way you are when you're teaching us."

"It really doesn't bother you, that she was a slave?"

Hollis ran his fingertip over the tabletop before replying. "I suppose it's hard for a nobleman to believe that I could care for somebody who's supposed to be beneath me, but I like Semeli—a lot—and that's what counts, ain't it? Besides, what real harm would it do? It's not as if I'm noble like you and Lady Gwyneth and have to marry to make alliances or increase my property or wealth, thank the Lord." He eyed Gavin thoughtfully. "I suppose you could say that in that way, I'm freer than you."

"Yes, you are freer than I am."

"Semeli's a wonderful girl I'm proud to know, and if she ever came to care—" He fell silent and blushed to the roots of his red hair before taking a deep breath and continuing. "Why should the world care what we do? Besides, Semeli will be the one who's making a sacrifice by caring for me."

"Because she was born a Persian princess?"

For a moment, Gavin thought Hollis had lost his senses as he threw back his head and laughed.

"I'm sorry, Gavin," Hollis said as he sobered, "I thought Gwyneth would have told you by now."

Gavin lowered his brows as he prepared to hear something else he should have been told.

"Semeli was no more born a Persian princess than I was," Hollis explained. "She just says that to strangers because they stare at her. She and her mother were brought here by a Norseman, a gift for the earl. The Norseman claimed he fathered her, and a big, strong brute he was." Hollis's lip curled with disgust. "I gather the earl wasn't impressed with the way the brute treated her mother, so he accepted the 'gift,' then told the Norseman he never wanted the man to set foot on his land again."

This version of Semeli's history sounded plausible, especially when Gavin recalled Semeli's muscular arms.

"She and Lady Gwyneth have been thick as thieves ever since."

Gavin squirmed at Hollis's offhand remark, then reminded himself Hollis didn't know who he really was. "I thought they seemed close, for maid and mistress."

"God save you, yes! They're friends, really, but Semeli—I told you she was proud—insists that she be *allowed* to do her work. She owes it to the earl, she says." Hollis sighed, and a nostalgic expression spread over his face. "I wish you could have been here with us when we were younger, Gavin," he said as if referring to a time long, long ago, "back when the earl was hale and hearty, and before Gwyneth's brother died. Oh, the times we had, I can tell you!" He chuckled. "By the saints, Gwyneth could get up to mischief. She could run like the wind and talk her way out of nearly anything, so she wasn't often punished."

He grinned at Gavin, then frowned, obviously misinterpreting the look on his companion's face. "Oh, she never did anything really bad, or hurt anybody. She'd just get these incredible ideas that sounded wonderful and fun at the time. Many a time, though, they'd turn out a bit . . . well, disastrous."

Gavin subdued the urge to share Lady Gwyneth's latest wonderful idea that also had the potential for turning into a disaster. "I can believe that."

Hollis shifted so that he was looking directly into Gavin's face. "Nobody wants to see her married to DeVilliers, especially her father. He hates DeVilliers. Always has, and DeVilliers knows it. Fortunately for us, Lord William kept in King Richard's good graces, although the taxes cost him dear."

Gavin had heard that King Richard the Lionhearted had always needed money. That was hard to believe about a king, but apparently his ill-fated crusade that did not lead to the recapture of Jerusalem from the Infidels, then his capture by Duke Leopold of Austria, who had turned him over to be ransomed by the German emperor, had required a huge sum. Many of the nobles in England had been forced to come up with the money, and they had done so—or rather, their tenants had, in raised rents and taxes.

"But now Richard's brother John is on the throne," Gavin noted.

"Aye, and he's a different animal entirely. He's waited years for his chance, and he's only too happy to help those who befriended him when Richard ruled. DeVilliers was one of them, so he's got the upper hand now. If he wants Gwyneth, I think John will make sure he gets her. You've never met DeVilliers, have you?"

"No, I haven't," Gavin replied. That was true. He had only seen him.

"He's a handsome devil, but a devil just the same. If half of what we hear about him is true, it'll be a sad day for us all if Gwyneth is forced to marry him."

"I suppose it would be."

Hollis inched closer and got a conspiratorial look in his eye. "Gwyneth likes you, Gavin. She's trying not to show it, but I know her too well. I think you like her, too, don't you?"

"Yes, I like her."

"Gavin, are you, um, betrothed?"

Gavin abruptly sat back on his bench. He had said enough already, and he could guess where this was going.

"I didn't mean to intrude. It's just that all the men admire and respect you, and we all hate DeVilliers, and

Gwyneth likes you, and—"

And they had talked enough about Lady Gwyneth and her future in which he could have no part.

"Lord William needs to have good food," he interrupted after taking a quick look around to make sure no one was within earshot. "Lady Gwyneth has no meat, nor money to buy any, so I am organizing a little hunt."

Hollis's eyes widened and he slid forward on his elbows until he and Gavin were nearly nose to nose, all thought of Lady Gwyneth's possible marriage plans clearly forgotten.

Thank God.

"Poaching?" Hollis repeated in a whisper that was more keen and curious than shocked and horrified, Gavin was pleased to note.

He nodded.

"The baron's lands are best for that."

It seemed Emlyn wasn't the only one who had done a little illegal hunting before. "Really?"

"Aye. I know them well. When do you want to go?"

"Dawn tomorrow?"

"Fine by me, my friend."

Hollis could have no idea how pleased and happy that simple address made him. "The weather should hold, I think," Gavin said. "Emlyn will come, too."

"Ah, then we'll get something for certain. Where do we meet?"

"Where do you think would be best?"

"There's an old hut near the mill."

"I know the mill."

"Then you'll find the hut."

Gavin smiled. So did Hollis.

Sally came toward the table carrying a tray bearing mugs and meat pies. "Eat up, both of you. From what I hear, you've had a busy time of it these days."

They did as she'd suggested, and Gavin discovered a savory beef pie with plenty of gravy was one of the best things he had ever tasted. Hollis likewise tucked in with hearty appetite, and soon both of them were sated nearly to bursting, only a bit of ale left in their mugs.

With a contented sigh, Gavin thanked Hollis for the meal. "I shall be sorry to see you go, Hollis."

"And I will be sorry to leave, but I don't have much choice, not if I want to make something of myself without my stepfather hounding me night and day and insulting Semeli every chance he gets. Now that I know how to use a sword and spear and protect myself, thanks to you, I've decided to become a soldier. I'll head for London and see if I can find a place in the army of one of the men of the king's court." He cocked his head as he looked at Gavin. "I don't suppose Sir Henry would be needin' men?"

"He might," Gavin cautiously allowed. "Lady Gwyneth might need you more."

"Aye, that's what Semeli said. She's angry with me about it, but I'm only thinking of us." He looked beseechingly at Gavin. "You understand, don't you? I've got to go. When I've got some money, and a place in the world, I'll come back. I've asked Semeli to wait." His voice fell. "I pray she will."

Gavin reached out and put a hand on his friend's shoulder. "I think she will."

Indeed, he couldn't fault Hollis for his solution to what seemed an insurmountable obstacle. In fact, he envied him the freedom he had as an honest man, which was something Gavin had never really known. He had been in the gallows' shadow for as long as he could remember, for he had been stealing for as long as he could remember.

Nevertheless, he began to wonder what kind of soldier *he* would make.

Soldiers were knighted on the battlefield sometimes and knights could win prizes and estates in tournaments . . . but that could take years. Despite that, he was tempted to ask Hollis if he could go with him—except then he would have to tell Hollis the truth about who he was and what he had done in his life. He couldn't claim to be a squire if he was to become a common foot soldier.

Suddenly Gavin *wanted* to tell Hollis the truth. He wanted to tell his friend everything, about his past and his hopes for the future.

But he didn't dare. The truth—or the revelation of the lies he had told—would surely destroy the bond of friendship between them.

He did not want to lose that, so for as long as he could, he would be Gavin of Inverlea.

However short a time that might prove to be.

CHAPTER FOURTEEN

That evening, Gwyneth sat beside Gavin at the evening meal. He wasn't very hungry, and she wondered if it was because he was worried about the poaching. She was tense about that, too, and the fact that Semeli was not in the hall.

Semeli was rarely ill, and she had said nothing about feeling unwell that day.

"I have spoken with Emlyn, and he has agreed to come with me," Gavin whispered as he finished eating a piece of bread.

"That's good," she replied, relieved. "You should be successful, then."

She likewise tore off a piece of bread and dipped it into the thin soup, all that was left of the last of the chickens.

"Hollis is coming, too. They both say the baron's wood is the best place."

That got her full attention. "The baron's wood? And Hollis is going, too?"

Gavin nodded. "I gather Hollis knows that wood well."

She could not argue with that. She and Hollis and Semeli had spent hours there in their childhood, delighted to think they were on land they should avoid. "When do you go?"

"First light. We meet at the hut near the mill. There is something more."

She eyed him warily.

"I thought somebody was spying on the men practicing from the riverbank."

She stiffened, fear slithering along her spine. She should not have assumed that just because De Villiers had not come by, he wasn't curious about what was happening at Haverleigh.

Rufus seemed to sense her dismay, for he sat up and whined. "Who was it?" she asked, petting Rufus's head to quiet him.

"I don't know, and I can't even be sure there was anybody there. I saw something for only a brief moment, and later the ground was too muddy for me to tell if it had been men or animals. Nevertheless, I thought you would want to know."

"Yes," she agreed, even as her stomach seemed filled with lead. Her plan had been successful so far, and she had allowed herself to forget that the longer Gavin stayed, the riskier it was for him, and for her, too.

As for the poaching, she had better make sure it was as safe as possible for all concerned, and she knew one way to make that so.

"I'm sorry to upset you," Gavin said softly, almost tenderly.

The gentle tone of his voice thrilled her as much as his kiss had.

Yes, he had to leave Haverleigh soon, before her feelings became even stronger. Before she wanted to beg him to say.

No, she already wanted to do that. Before she *did* beg him to stay.

Indeed, if she were really thinking of what was best for Gavin, she would tell him to go now.

But she simply could not bring herself to do it. Once the poaching was finished, once her father had the necessary food, *then* she would order Gavin to go. "If you will excuse me, I should find Semeli."

She didn't wait for his answer, but rose and hurried to the large room that all the women servants shared. A row of beds lined the chamber, each with a chest at the foot where the women kept their personal belongings.

Curled into a ball, Semeli lay on her side, her back to the door.

"Are you ill?" Gwyneth asked softly as she sat beside her friend. Her weight made the ropes holding the straw mattress squeak a little. "Semeli, what is it?"

Her friend buried her head farther into her goosedown pillow, hiding her face. "Nothing, my lady, nothing. I shall be all right in the morning."

My lady? Semeli rarely called her that, and it sounded like she was weeping. Something terrible must have happened to hurt or upset her. "Are you . . . are you crying?"

"Please, my lady, go away."

Go away? The harsh words pierced Gwyneth to the heart, especially since there was one thing that could account for it, one thing that filled her with guilt and would explain why her friend wanted her to leave.

Semeli must have discovered that she had been keeping the truth about Gavin from her.

Or maybe not, Gwyneth thought, desperately hoping that Semeli's pain was not her fault. Thomas hated her and never lost an opportunity to let her know it. And it was no secret that she liked Hollis. Maybe Hollis had said or done something to distress her. "Please tell me what's happened, Semeli. I want to help."

"No," came the muffled reply. "It is nothing."

Gwyneth leaned closer, even more worried and guilt ridden. "Aren't we friends, Semeli? Aren't I more than your mistress? If that's so, won't you tell me what's upset you?"

Even as she asked Semeli, Gwyneth feared it was a mistake. After all, if Semeli suspected she had not been honest about Gavin, what was she going to say? She yearned to confide in her friend, but if DeVilliers was spying on them, he wouldn't for long. Soon enough he would ride through the gates and demand to know what was happening, or perhaps even insist upon taking charge. If that happened, the less Semeli knew, the better.

At last Semeli rolled over onto her back, wiped her cheeks, and sat up, hugging her knees. "I am not a Persian princess. I do not even know where Persia really is. I was born a slave, the daughter of a slave stolen from the lands across the southern sea."

"I know," Gwyneth answered, puzzled.

"Thomas hates me."

This was nothing Gwyneth did not already know, either. "He's suspicious of anybody who isn't from Haverleigh," she said, her loathing of Thomas growing even more. He must be the cause of this. Perhaps her father would soon be well enough that she could suggest a new reeve. Thomas could keep excellent accounts, but he was a bully, too.

Semeli glumly shook her head. "He *loathes* me, and you know it as well as I. He thinks I am not worthy to . . . to talk to Hollis."

"What did he say?" Gwyneth demanded, her outrage growing. "I'll speak to him tomorrow. He cannot—"

Semeli took hold of her hand. "Sit, my lady, please."

At the sight of Semeli's determined sincerity, Gwyneth did as she'd requested, the use of the formal address still disturbing.

"Say nothing to Thomas," Semeli urged. "Say nothing

to Hollis. Thomas is right. I am unworthy."

Gwyneth was so agitated, she jumped to her feet, unable to keep still. "No, you're not! You're my friend, and—"

"I am your servant first, although you allow me to be your friend."

"Semeli, I do not *allow* it! I am grateful for it. You honor me with your friendship. In that, we are equals."

"If you think so, you are the only one who does."

Gwyneth sat beside her friend. "I'm sure Hollis knows how much your friendship means to me."

"Hollis is leaving Haverleigh."

Gwyneth stared, aghast. "I don't believe it! Hollis wouldn't leave you, or Haverleigh."

Semeli nodded slowly. "Yes, he will, and soon. He has decided to be a soldier."

Gwyneth couldn't believe that, either. "A soldier? Hollis?"

"Since he has learned to fight, he thinks he can earn a good living in a knight's guard or a lord's army, perhaps even in the king's company."

Gwyneth had not foreseen this, and if she had, she would have done things differently, knowing her best friend's broken heart might be the price. She would have called for men of a certain age—older, certainly, than Hollis. "Is that all he said?"

"He says when he has enough money, he will come back. He . . . he has asked me to wait for him."

"Why, there! You see?" she cried, relieved as some of her faith in Hollis's good nature returned to her, and her guilt diminished a little. "He does care for you, and he . . ." Her words trailed off at Semeli's stricken expression.

"He says that now, but he will meet other girls, girls who were not born slaves. Girls Thomas would approve of. Girls who will want him, and then he will forget all about me."

"Oh, that's not true!" Gwyneth protested, even as she wondered if Gavin would forget *her*. "He'll come back. I know he will. He won't break his word, and he cares nothing for his stepfather, or his stepfather's opinions. You know that as well as I do."

"Part of me says I should tell him not to come back, that he will be happier if he does not."

"That's impossible! He cares about you too much, Semeli," Gwyneth cried, believing it with all her heart.

"You cannot understand. People will look down on him the way Thomas does if Hollis comes back for me or if we try to make a life together. I do not want him to suffer because of me."

"He won't."

"You have not walked alone through the village as I have. You have not seen the sly looks, the questioning glances, the curled lips. You have not heard the things people say. You have not endured the scorn. I have, my lady, and they will look on Hollis the same way if he . . . if he loves me." She sighed wearily. "In my heart I think I always knew this day would come, and I have dreaded it. But now it is here, and so it must be."

Gwyneth wanted to deny everything Semeli said, to tell her that nobody hated her simply because of her birth. But although that was horrible and unfair, she could not. Semeli was right. She and Hollis were from two different classes, just as Gwyneth and Gavin were. Society had harsh words for those who tried to rise above the class into which they'd been born. It was the way of things, no matter how much she wished it were not. To defy society would take strength and power and position. They were girls in a world ruled by men, and there was nothing they could do.

"But oh, Gwyneth, I love Hollis," Semeli whispered, her eyes filling with tears as she laid her head on her knees. "I don't want him to go."

Gwyneth knew exactly how she felt as she put her arms around her friend and laid her head against Semeli's.

Tears filled her eyes, not solely because of her friend's sorrow. At least Semeli could speak of the person she cared about. Gwyneth could not. Not to Semeli. Not to her father.

Not even to herself. She dared not admit the feelings

that had taken root in her heart for a young man who was but a common thief, even if he was more truly noble and honorable than many a man claimed to be.

"Do you truly think he will return to me?" Semeli whispered as she wept.

"I *know* it!" Gwyneth said fervently, even as her tears spilled onto her cheeks.

She did not wipe them away. Here, now, she would indulge in the sorrow she shared with her friend, even if it wasn't quite the same.

For Semeli could at least hope for a future with the man she loved.

Desmond DeVilliers sat alone in his solar, using the tip of his dagger to clean the dirt from beneath his fingernails. The scent of a multitude of expensive beeswax candles filled the air, and their illumination made the jeweled rings on his fingers sparkle and gleam with every swift, small movement of his hands.

His attention was not really on his task. He was thinking about Thomas, and the report the man had made that day about the training at Haverleigh before he'd gone on his way to Salisbury. It seemed the young squire had indeed accomplished wonders.

Well, DeVilliers consoled himself, Thomas was only a merchant who had achieved a small level of importance.

Who was he to judge the fighting capability of farmers and boys?

Nevertheless, perhaps it was time to make another journey to Haverleigh to see for himself. He wasn't keen to meet any squire of Sir Henry D'Argent's face-to-face, yet it might be worse to let this foolishness of Gwyneth's go on much longer.

There was a sudden flurry of footsteps on the stairs leading to his solar. DeVilliers jumped to his feet and faced the door, his dagger at the ready, as a fist pounded on it. "Who is it?" he demanded.

"Rolf," his sergeant-at-arms called out.

Relaxing, DeVilliers sheathed his dagger in his belt and strode to the door. He threw it open and glared at Rolf. A group of his regular soldiers stood behind the sergeant, their faces expressionless in the light of the torches in the brackets on the wall. "Well, what is so important that you come charging up the stairs as if we're under attack?"

His soldiers shoved three men forward. The two short, stocky ones cowered like rats, but the one in front tall, thin, and with a long, curving scar on his cheek—seemed to have a bit more backbone. All three looked as dishonest as it was possible for men to be.

"Caught stealing, were they?" he guessed. He waved his hand as he would if a fly were buzzing about him. "Hang them."

"No, my lord, no!" the tall, scarred one cried. "We ain't stolen nothing. We come of our own free will. We've got somethin' important to tell ya."

"What can such rogues possibly have to say that could be important to me?"

"It's about that squire there at Haverleigh."

DeVilliers moved away from the door. "Bring them in."

They did, and Rolf forced the three men to their knees.

Ignoring the stench of their unwashed clothes and bodies, DeVilliers circled around them, then went behind his desk to sit as if in judgment. "So, what is this important information about the squire at Haverleigh you have to tell me?"

"I . . ." The tall man wet his lips nervously, then stuck out his chin. "I think it's worth something."

DeVilliers nodded at Rolf, who cuffed the man hard on his ear.

"I will decide if information is worth something, not you," DeVilliers said sternly. "If you don't tell me what you know, I'll have you killed."

The man raised his eyes, and to his surprise, DeVilliers saw a defiant gleam. "If you don't pay up, you won't find out why we marched up t' the gate and asked to see you."

This man really believed that what he had to say was worth defying a Norman nobleman. More than that, he also obviously believed it was worth money. "Who are you?"

"I'm Fulk, and this is Drogo and Bert." Drogo and Bert nodded. Then they went back to looking like dogs who had been beaten. "We, um, we travel about, my lord, and in our travels, we meet lots of people. Good ones, bad ones. You know how it is."

"Thank God, I do not," DeVilliers answered. "However, if I were to guess, Fulk, I would say that you are an example of one of the bad ones."

Fulk shrugged. "Well, I won't claim to be perfect."

Impudent dog. He should be hanged just for his manner. "Wise of you."

"But I ain't done nothin' on your estate, my lord."

"Again, that's wise of you."

"And what I got to say you'll be glad to hear."

"So you keep implying. Now, what is it you have to tell me?"

Fulk got to his feet. Rolf stepped forward, obviously intending to force him to his knees again, but DeVilliers shook his head. This man's rudeness was amusing, in a way, since he could have him killed as easily as another man took a sip of water.

"That squire ain't no more noble born than I am," Fulk declared. "He's a gutter-born brat, and a thief to boot."

DeVilliers stared at him, then, enraged at the man's

audacity, slowly rose. "That is the most outrageous lie any-one has ever dared to tell me to my face."

The rogue met his glare steadily. "It ain't a lie. It's the truth. If you talk to him, you'll know it right enough, my lord. He might be able to fool common folk and a girl, but he surely couldn't trick *you*."

DeVilliers took a deep breath and fought to control his anger and think. If this lout was lying, he wouldn't be so bold—or would he? Yet if this was true, here was the way to gain control of Gwyneth, and Haverleigh. The earl was still unwell, and every noble in England would agree that a girl who could be tricked by a thief should not have command of an estate. But he could not move on the word of men such as these. "Gwyneth might be a foolish, stub-born girl, but I never thought she was stupid."

"Oh, he's a clever one, my lord. Very clever."

"What about this training he's supposed to be doing?"

Fulk sniffed. "If you can call it that. He's showing them how to brawl, more like. I been a soldier myself, my lord, and he don't know how to fight proper."

"How is it you know him?"

"We, um, met him before, see. In Salisbury. He was pickin' pockets there and braggin' about it." Fulk turned to Drogo and Bert. "Ain't that right, boys?"

They nodded. "Aye, braggin'," Drogo muttered.

"And pickin' pockets," Bert confirmed.

"He's a good-lookin' fella, my lord, and smart as they come, so it's no wonder to me he's fooled the young lady and those peasants."

DeVilliers regarded Fulk and the others a moment. "I shall go to Haverleigh tomorrow and meet this squire for myself. You will come, too. Rolf, have these men taken to the dungeon."

"My lord!" Fulk protested.

"What you've told me is worthless until I am convinced of the truth of it. In the meantime, you will enjoy the hospitality of my castle as I see fit."

CHAPTER FIFTEEN

The sky in the east was barely light when Gavin awoke. He climbed out of his warm bed, dressed quickly in a dark brown woolen tunic that had been Rylan's, black breeches and boots, then went to the window. No clouds hid the dimming stars. A slight mist covered the meadow nearest the river. It seemed a perfect early morn for hunting or poaching.

Or spying.

Had someone been watching them from the river? If so, who had it been? Had DeVilliers learned what he was doing and sent men to see? Had he been wrong to think Fulk and the others would leave without making sure he was dead?

He ran his hand through his hair. The longer he stayed here, the more dangerous it was. He should leave as soon as possible. He had trained the men the best he could. There was nothing more to keep him here . . . except Gwyneth, and that was the worst reason of all to stay.

Sighing at the hopelessness of feelings he could no longer deny for a girl as far above him as the angels in heaven, he turned to find Gwyneth standing on the threshold of his chamber, oddly dressed in a shortened gown with breeches showing beneath. She had a bow in her hands and a quiver attached to her belt. Behind her was Semeli, likewise oddly attired, and with a sheathed dagger hanging from the belt about her waist.

"What are you doing here, my lady, and armed?" he asked after the initial shock had passed. "Are those breeches you're wearing, and Semeli, too?"

"We're coming with you."

Dumbfounded, he stared at her in disbelief, until the resolute expression in her eyes confirmed that she was perfectly serious. "I don't think you should," he protested. "It's too dangerous."

"You and the others are breaking the law for my father's sake, so I believe it only right that I share that risk. If you are caught by DeVilliers's men, I can tell them—and DeVilliers, if necessary—that you are in the wood on my orders. You said having a squire with them would protect them, and you're right. I also think I might be even more valuable in that regard. And I *am* a fine shot with a bow."

"What about Semeli?" he demanded. "She shouldn't—"

If Semeli's eyes had been daggers, he'd have been dead. "I am not afraid of danger."

"I still don't think—"

"I am not asking your opinion, Gavin," Gwyneth interrupted. "I am *telling* you we are going, and you cannot stop me."

"Fine," Gavin retorted, throwing up his hands in exasperation as Semeli's gaze flicked from Gwyneth back to him. "If you don't want to listen to me and insist on putting yourselves in danger, so be it." He reached for his sword belt and buckled it around his waist. "Where's Rufus?"

"He's not a hunting hound. He's staying with my father."

"I see." He strode past them out onto the landing, and trotted down the steps, leaving Gwyneth and Semeli to hurry along behind.

Gwyneth scowled. He was being such a . . . such a *man*! As arrogant as the baron, as annoying as Thomas, as condescending as . . . as . . . well, most of the men she had ever met! He was probably just jealous of her skill.

Well, she would show him skill!

"Don't let him bother you," she muttered under her breath as they crossed the courtyard, panting a little from the effort of trying to keep up with Gavin's long strides that had taken him ahead of them.

"What did you say?"

"Nothing, Semeli. I was just thinking out loud."

"Well, I am going to be talking out loud and telling Gavin to slow down or I will be without breath entirely," Semeli complained as they passed through the gate.

This morning it was a good thing they had no sentries. It spared any explanation as to where they were going, and so early, or why.

"If you complain, he'll say we aren't fit to go along with them," Gwyneth warned.

"You are the lady of Haverleigh. He is but a guest. He cannot stop you."

"He might decide to try," she replied as they hurried though the sleeping village.

They spoke no more because of Gavin's quick pace, and soon enough they saw the hut near the mill on the river, as well as the two young men waiting beside it.

Hollis and Emlyn spotted them, and she could see that they were as puzzled as Gavin had been. He reached them first, and she watched him gesture at them, his movements brisk and annoyed.

"As I told Gavin, I won't let you all put yourselves in danger and not share it," she said as she and Semeli joined them and before they could protest.

Emlyn fingered his bowstring. "Well, I'm thinking that's not a bad idea. If we're caught, I'll be glad you're with us."

"Exactly," Gwyneth replied. "Hollis?"

"I'm not so sure it's safe, but since you're here and so insistent . . ." He shrugged and smiled at Semeli.

"I still think letting them come along is a mistake," Gavin muttered.

"How unfortunate for you, because we're going with

you whether you like it or not," Gwyneth snapped. "Now, are we going hunting, or are we going to stand here and argue about it all day?"

Scowling, Gavin turned to Hollis. "Lead the way."

Hollis started off through the trees, Emlyn and Gavin behind him, while Gwyneth and Semeli brought up the rear. The scent of damp earth rose up around them, and the undergrowth rustled as they brushed by. The air was still, save for bird song and the harsh caw of crows in the meadow a short distance away. Occasionally a squirrel scampered across a branch overhead and some other small creature scurried close by, but generally the wood was as hushed as an empty cathedral.

After a while, Hollis came to a halt. "There is a little spring just past here where animals come to drink," he said quietly. "I think if we wait here, something worth taking will come. Emlyn, you go behind that tree. Semeli and I will hide behind this big rock. Gwyneth, why don't you and Gavin go on the other side of the stream and keep watch? You can whistle if you see something coming from that direction."

"I don't know how to whistle," Gavin admitted with obvious reluctance.

He was sulking like a big baby because she had overruled him and come along despite his objections. "I do," she said, ignoring Gavin.

Hollis grinned. "There, now. Easy as can be, isn't it?"

"Why don't you and I keep watch, and Semeli and Gwyneth can wait behind the rock?" Gavin suggested.

Hollis and Semeli exchanged glances.

This was ridiculous, Gwyneth thought, annoyed. They had a job to do, and it wasn't important if Gavin didn't want to be with her.

"What does it matter who waits with whom?" she demanded.

Gavin gave an infuriating shrug of his broad shoulders. "As you wish, my lady."

"Then come along," she ordered, marching ahead and pausing on the bank of the stream to make sure Gavin was following. When she saw that he was, she jumped across the clear water babbling over the rocky bed as it made its way toward the river.

She went behind a prickly holly bush as tall as Gavin, and laying her bow beside her, crouched down to peer through the pointed leaves and branches. Hollis and Semeli disappeared behind the rock, and Emlyn was barely visible behind a tree. His bow stuck out a bit, and there was an arrow already nocked and ready to shoot.

She didn't look at Gavin as he joined her. Why should she? They were supposed to be looking for game, not at each other.

Out of the corner of her eye, however, she saw him

sit on a nearby stump and rest one foot on his knee, as casual as you please.

What else should she expect? He was used to breaking the law. He did it all the time, whereas she could feel the sweat trickling down her back. Her nervousness had nothing to do with him sitting calmly behind her and watching her, either.

"Your legs will ache if you stay in that position for much longer," he whispered after a while.

In truth, her legs *were* starting to ache, but she wasn't about to admit that to *him*.

"The ground is too damp to sit on," she answered, likewise in a whisper.

"You could sit on that stump there." He pointed to one a short distance away.

"Then I wouldn't be able to see the stream."

"I'll tell you if I see something, and you can whistle."

"If you persist in whispering," she hissed, "you'll frighten the animals away."

"Fine," he muttered under his breath. "Let your limbs ache." He picked up a stick and started to peel off the bark.

He said not another word, and she told herself she was glad. She kept her gaze on the stream as if unable to look at anything else. He found a few more sticks and peeled off their bark.

Suddenly, Gavin jumped to his feet. Before she could

ask him what in the name of the saints he thought he was doing, he marched toward her and pulled her to her feet.

Her limbs were so stiff, she fairly screamed in agony, but the intense, questioning look in Gavin's eyes kept her from complaining. "Are you always this stubborn?" he demanded in a harsh whisper.

She shoved him back and rubbed her legs. She spoke quietly but firmly. "As I keep trying to get through that head of yours, we don't want to frighten the animals away."

"You could have changed your position. I bet you would have except that you want to show me what a strong, determined girl you are." He put his hands on his hips. "Well, you have."

"As long as my father is ill, I am the commander of Haverleigh," she retorted, still whispering as she pointed at her chest, "and if I want to go poaching, I will!"

Gavin glared at her.

She glared right back, her breathing fast and shallow.

As was his.

He stepped closer.

She didn't step back.

He took hold of her by the arms.

She didn't move.

He didn't kiss her. Instead, he said softly, "Yes, you are the commander of Haverleigh. I can even admire your notion of honor, that you won't let your people risk more than you are willing to. But it's also true that you don't belong in the woods, poaching. What about your responsibilities to the rest of your tenants? What if we are caught?"

"Of course I've thought about that," she retorted just as quietly, all the while trying to ignore the feel of his hands on her arms. His lean, strong fingers. The warmth that bloomed within her when he touched her, even this way. "I explained why I came, and any punishment DeVilliers decides is necessary will have to be done to me as well, so he will probably let you all go free."

Gavin's gaze still bored into her, as if he were trying to read her mind. "Or he might want something in exchange for our freedom?"

She flushed and couldn't look into Gavin's piercing brown eyes.

He put his knuckle under her chin and gently raised her face so she had to look at him. "He'll want *you*, won't he?"

She didn't answer him directly. "Please let go of me, Gavin."

He did, his hands falling limply at his side.

"Yes, DeVilliers wants me for his wife," she admitted, not meeting Gavin's worried gaze, "and Haverleigh in his grasp. He always has." She turned away, her whole body shaking with suppressed emotion. "I *hate* him."

Gavin came up behind her and lightly laid his hands on her shoulders. "Yet you would risk hastening a marriage to him by coming with us?" he asked, his warm breath brushing her cheek.

She swallowed hard. "For my friends, of course I would."

There was a long moment of silence. Tension seemed to stretch between them as she waited for him to move or speak. At last he did. "Am I your friend, too, then, Gwyneth?"

She didn't answer. She couldn't, because she didn't want him for a friend. She wanted . . . something more.

He turned her so that she faced him and the anguished expression in his eyes smote her to the heart. "I don't want you to marry DeVilliers. Surely there are better noblemen who deserve you and would be rightly proud to win your love."

Had he truly no idea how she felt about him? "Gavin, I wish . . ." She took a deep breath, then risked having her feelings known, her yearnings made plain, the truth revealed. "I wish that there could be more between us. That we were equals in rank. That you really were a squire, or that I was a peasant's daughter."

His incredulous gaze searched her face, and he was scarcely breathing. "You . . . you do?"

She nodded once, and her arms slipped around his

waist. "Especially when you kiss me, I wish it with all my heart."

They looked at one another for a long moment, both realizing the depth of their feelings, and the hopelessness of them.

Gavin drew her close. "Run away with me, Gwyneth."

For a moment, it was as if everything had stopped: her heartbeat, the birds singing, the stream burbling past. The vista of a future with Gavin seemed to open before her eyes and "Yes!" came to her lips.

But then the image of her father and the home she would have to leave behind burst in upon her. The vision of a future with Gavin melted away, to be replaced by the harsh realities of duty and obligation, based on a different kind of love. "I cannot leave my father."

His soft brown eyes sad but accepting, Gavin brushed a lock of hair from her cheek, that little caress making it even harder for her to refuse what he had suggested. "I should have realized that."

She took his hand, warm and strong, and held it against her cheek. "I couldn't leave him, or my people, or they will come under DeVilliers's rule sooner."

Gavin smiled wistfully and covered her hand with his. "I understand. Besides, what could I offer you except a life of poverty and hardship? Even if I could find work somewhere, I could never be more than a common laborer."

"I don't think you would ever be a common anything,

Gavin, and if I had only myself to think about . . ."

"You'd really consider coming with me?"

She nodded.

His arms slipped around her and he pulled her close. Then he lowered his head and kissed her.

She turned into him, giving herself up to the delight of it, even though deep inside she felt a sadness such as she had never known. No matter how much she wished it could be otherwise, he could never be more to her than a youth who had helped her, once upon a time.

His mouth soft and gentle, he deepened his kiss and she relaxed, her arms holding him closer. She would gladly, gladly stay here all day if she could be with him like this, kissing him and being kissed.

And then a shout pierced the stillness.

CHAPTER SIXTEEN

Emlyn cried out again as something crashed through the underbrush near the river. Gavin and Gwyneth gasped, then ran at once to help, Gwyneth pausing only long enough to snatch up her bow.

They halted as a huge boar with horrible tusks that could slice through a man's flesh ran past Emlyn directly at them. Its small eyes were almost invisible in its dark hide, and its thick, bristled tail lashed like a snake. One of Emlyn's arrows stuck out of its shoulder, yet still it came on.

Gwyneth reached for an arrow just as Gavin shoved her out of the way, rolling with her in the dirt. Emlyn shouted again, and another arrow whizzed through the air. The boar, a few yards away, squealed and thrashed on the ground, the arrow in its back. It got to its feet as Hollis appeared, a drawn knife in his hands. He tackled the boar, but it twisted, narrowly missing him with its tusks. The knife flew out of Hollis's hands as he landed on his back with a thud.

As Gwyneth got to her feet, Gavin scrambled for Hollis's knife and grabbed it. The boar foamed at the mouth as it writhed in pain.

It was wounded and in agony and Gwyneth knew now it was at its most dangerous. It might do almost anything.

Her desperate gaze took in the scene before her. Hollis still lay on the ground, winded and perhaps hurt. Crouched, his knife in hand, Gavin kept his eyes on the boar. Semeli crept closer to it, holding her dagger raised, and Emlyn stood nearby trying to nock another arrow with trembling fingers.

He was shaking so much, his arrow would never fly true.

With a silent prayer, Gwyneth quickly nocked her arrow, took a deep breath, and aimed.

The enraged beast rushed at Gavin. He leaped out of its path, and as he did, she let her arrow fly. There was a high-pitched squeal, then the animal fell to the ground dead, her arrow through its eye.

For a long moment they were all too stunned to speak, the only sound that broke the forest's stillness was their labored breathing.

Gwyneth was the first to recover. She ran to Gavin and helped him to his feet.

"Are you hurt?" she cried when she saw blood on his tunic.

"No, I don't think so." His breathing hoarse, he

checked and shook his head. "None of the blood is mine."

As Hollis started to get up from the ground, Semeli sheathed her dagger and hurried to help him.

"You could have been killed, you bloody great dolt," she scolded. "Attacking that beast in such a manner—what were you thinking?"

She wasn't fooling anybody with her words, for her tone told them all she was more relieved than angry.

"That it was going for Gwyneth and Gavin," Hollis replied as he sat heavily on a nearby rock. "That's why you pulled your dagger, wasn't it? You were going for it, too, weren't you?"

Semeli's dusky cheeks flushed, and she criticized him no more.

Emlyn went to stand beside the dead boar. He stared down at it warily, as if he feared it might rise again.

"It's dead," Gavin assured him.

"I should have waited a bit longer before shooting," Emlyn murmured, nudging the beast with his toe. "Would have hit him in a better spot. Good thing you finally took a shot, my lady, but, um, I don't think you were watching very well, or you would have had more warning."

Gwyneth warmed with a blush. She wasn't ashamed she had been kissing Gavin. She was embarrassed that Emlyn had guessed they weren't watching as they should have been. "We were talking."

"Talking," Gavin confirmed, but he was blushing, too.

"Must have been an interesting conversation," Hollis noted with a grin.

"Aye, it was," Gavin said.

Blushing even more, Gwyneth tried to keep her mind on the task at hand. "How are we going to get it back to Haverleigh? I didn't think we would get anything so huge."

They all looked at the wild boar, which had to weigh at least two hundred pounds. One person couldn't possibly carry it.

"We could make a litter," Hollis suggested.

"Aye, we could," Emlyn seconded.

"People will know that we've been hunting if we come out of the forest dragging it," Gwyneth pointed out.

"We shall simply have to cut it up, take what we can, and leave the rest," Semeli said.

They all looked at her. "Well, what else can we do?" she asked, shrugging her shoulders with a motion like a ripple.

"If you give me the dagger, I'll do the butchering," Gavin offered after they silently acknowledged that Semeli was right. "What will we carry the meat in?"

Semeli pulled out some sacks she had tucked into her belt. "I thought we might catch birds or rabbits."

"All right, then," Gavin replied. "Why don't you girls start back to Haverleigh and let us bring the meat to Etienne?"

As tempting as that was, Gwyneth thought of something else. "You'll get more blood on your clothes if you butcher it."

"You're right." Gavin stripped off his tunic. He didn't even shiver in the cool morning air.

"I'll wash that out." Gwyneth said. "We should do it here, before we go back, or it will be obvious we were hunting."

With a nod, Gavin tossed her the tunic.

"I do not wish to see any more of that creature than I have to, so I will go with you to the stream," Semeli announced.

Glad of her company, Gwyneth led the way to the river and dipped the blood-splattered garment into the freezing water. Behind them, they could hear the quiet discussion as the others decided how they were going to butcher the boar.

Semeli crouched beside her. "I'll wash it."

"No, I don't mind."

"I thought that boar was going to kill Hollis, and Gavin, too."

"I was afraid for them, as well." Gwyneth eyed her friend. "Would you really have tried to kill it with Rylan's dagger?"

"Yes."

They were silent for a moment as Gwyneth continued

to swirl the garment in the water. Then she slid her friend another sidelong glance. "I think Gavin and I weren't the only ones not keeping as good a watch as we should have."

Semeli tossed her head. "I am thinking that Hollis may come back to me after all."

Gwyneth smiled, happy for her. "I'm sure he will." She grew serious as she compared her friend's possible future with her own. "I envy you that hope, Semeli."

Semeli put her hand on Gwyneth's shoulder. "Gavin is a fine young man. Lord William will surely think so, too. I know you like each other. Perhaps someday Gavin, too, will come back."

"I'm sure he has other obligations." Gwyneth lied, hating herself for doing so, but seeing no alternative.

"Well, of course he does, as all noblemen must." Semeli frowned. "He is not already betrothed, is he?"

"We have not discussed it," Gwyneth replied.

Semeli looked at her strangely, and Gwyneth's heart sank. She was sure Semeli guessed that she wasn't being completely honest.

"I would . . . I would rather not talk about that," she said, looking away.

Semeli sighed. "I know you have many cares, so I will say no more."

Gwyneth sighed, and smiled tremulously before she

looked back over her shoulder at the boys. "I think they're nearly finished."

As they rose, a sound drifted to them on the wind, of horses' hooves and the jingling of chain mail—the unmistakable sounds of a troop of mounted soldiers. It came from the road leading through the forest a short distance away.

Gwyneth snatched up the wet tunic and hurried back to the others as quickly and silently as she could, with Semeli right behind.

Hollis pointed at the sacks. They were now a dark, disgusting red, as was the blade of the dagger in Gavin's hand. "All fin—"

"Shhhh!" Gwyneth hissed, putting her fingers to her lips to silence him.

She tossed the tunic to Gavin, who looked as shocked as Hollis and Emlyn.

"A troop of soldiers, not far off," she explained, whispering and pointing in the direction of the noise.

Gavin shoved the dagger into his breeches and tugged on his wet tunic, regardless of its dampness.

"Who do you think it is?" Emlyn asked in a hushed voice.

"Does it matter?" Gwyneth replied, picking up her bow. "Come on!"

The sound of men's voices, louder and nearer now, reached their ears, and they instinctively dropped like stones to the ground.

"Poachers, most like, my lord," a man called out. "The woodcutters don't come this way. Ground's too soft, especially in the spring."

Gwyneth raised her head and looked in the direction of the voice. A man was standing not far off to the east of them, peering through the branches. Another man came up behind him.

DeVilliers. Tall, arrogant, dressed in his customary black, his long cloak swirling about his booted ankles, he had never looked more like a crow than he did then, his narrow eyes peering through the trees. The hilt of his sword gleamed dully through the opening of his cloak.

In that moment, all Gwyneth's notions about being able to protect Gavin and the others by her presence alone seemed utterly foolish. If they were caught anywhere near the bloodied carcass of the boar, she would be safe enough, as long as DeVilliers had hopes of obtaining Haverleigh by marriage to her. But the others even supposing he believed Gavin was a squire, DeVilliers would care only that they had killed game in his wood, and that was a crime.

She handed her bow to Semeli, who gave her a quizzical look. Not explaining, she crept closer to Gavin.

"Wait until I've led them away, then get back to Haverleigh as quick as you can," she whispered. "Tell

Etienne to say we slaughtered our last pig this morning, and warn him that we may have guests for the next meal. Then go to your chamber and don't come out until I send word it's safe or fetch you myself."

She didn't linger long enough for him to answer before she jumped up and ran toward the two men. Neither did she look back while she silently and fervently prayed that her friends would do as she'd said and take the time she intended to buy them.

DeVilliers stood not far from his guard, and a soldier held the bridle of the baron's black gelding. Behind them was a sight that made her blood run even colder: a troop of soldiers such as she had never seen with DeVilliers before, rough-looking, hardened men whose attitude, weapons, and faces all cried out that they were hired mercenaries—well-trained, ruthless men whose loyalty belonged to whoever paid them.

Fear filled her. When and why had DeVilliers started to hire mercenaries like that?

Yet that was not all, for in the midst of these men, she saw the three thieves who had been with Gavin.

Her steps faltered. Those thieves knew who Gavin really was, and DeVilliers was heading toward Haverleigh. The thieves must have told DeVilliers about Gavin if they were with his men and not rotting in DeVilliers's dungeon.

If DeVilliers knew about Gavin, she must protect him the best she could. She must keep him hidden and his presence a secret for as long as possible. He had risked his life for her, and she must ensure that he did not suffer for it.

A frown on his haughty, hawklike face, DeVilliers put his hands on his hips when he saw her approaching. His cloak flared out like a bat's wings as Gwyneth marched resolutely forth and she forced herself to smile.

"Lady Gwyneth, what are you doing in my wood?" the baron demanded as she came to a halt. His frown deepened as he made an arrogant little bow. "Surely you are not alone? Have you not even got your dog with you?"

As the three outlaws exchanged wary glances, Gwyneth was glad she had left Rufus at home. The thieves might have recognized him.

"Greetings, my lord," she replied. "I could not bear being cooped up inside Haverleigh this morning, so I thought I'd take a walk even though I have no soldiers for an escort. Rufus can make so much noise, and run about so wildly, I left him behind, as it was peace I sought. Your wood is surely safe, since you are so diligent in patrolling it, as your presence this morning attests."

She cast an understandably curious eye over his

mercenaries. Up close, they looked even more vicious. "I see you have hired some new men."

"Yes, I have. We live in dangerous times—so it is certainly not wise for you to be out alone. We are on our way to Haverleigh, so we shall escort you home."

"That will not be necessary, my lord."

"I must insist."

Gwyneth knew she must tread carefully where the baron was concerned, even if every part of her rebelled at DeVilliers's arrogant and presumptuous manner. "As you wish, my lord," she conceded.

"Come, my dear," he said, turning toward his horse. "You may ride with me."

She would rather crawl all the way to London, and the others needed time to get back. "It is a lovely morning, my lord. Can we not walk together? We so rarely have a chance to . . ."

She swallowed hard. Then, summoning every ounce of her determination, she batted her eyelashes and smiled again. ". . . To be alone together. Your men can follow some distance behind, can they not?"

His eyes narrowed. "Do you wish to be alone with me, my lady? This is an unexpected suggestion."

"As you no doubt know, my lord, King John has a way of forcing people to marry, and it has occurred to me that perhaps I should be happy that a man like you wishes to have me for his bride." She almost gagged on the words, but to keep him from suspecting that she was acting against him, she would tell DeVilliers what he would most like to hear.

DeVilliers smiled, a gleam of triumph and lust in his evil eyes that chilled her heart completely.

"I'm glad you're seeing reason at last," he said.

Although she detested even the brush of the fabric of his clothes against her, she slipped her arm through his. He covered her hand with his gloved one, making her feel as if he were already taking possession of her. "Since it is a lovely day, I will be delighted to walk the rest of the way to Haverleigh."

DeVilliers ran his gaze over her in a way that made her want to slap him. "Interesting wardrobe, my lady."

"Yes, isn't it? These garments are very comfortable," she answered.

After they had gone a little farther and were some distance ahead of his men, DeVilliers suddenly tugged her closer.

"Don't try to play the coy maiden with me now, Gwyneth," he said harshly in her ear. "I have heard some very disturbing reports about what has been going on at Haverleigh."

"I don't know what you're talking about. There has been nothing that should disturb you happening at Haverleigh," she replied as if utterly baffled and upset.

DeVilliers smiled slowly and with disdain in his dark

eyes—as if he had her completely in his power and her attempt to fool him amused him. "If you say so. I shall just have to wait and see what I find at Haverleigh, and in the meantime, enjoy this chance to walk through the wood in the company of a charming young lady."

CHAPTER SEVENTEEN

Gavin, Hollis, Emlyn, and Semeli took the meat to Etienne and told him to say it was a pig. Shocked, Etienne was speechless, but he nodded in understanding. Hollis and Emlyn took their leave and headed back to the village, while Semeli went to change her clothes.

Gavin hurried on to his chamber. He didn't want to hide like a criminal, but he *was* a criminal, when all was said and done, and surely if he was wise, he would do what Gwyneth said.

Yet what if Gwyneth was in danger?

Deep in thought, conjuring up a thousand worrisome images, he passed the earl's door as Rufus trotted out. The dog eagerly followed him, and he seemed to guess that something was wrong, for when they entered Gavin's chamber, Rufus kept nudging Gavin's leg as if asking him to explain.

Gavin stripped off his damp tunic and put on the expensive one. Then, worrying and wondering what had happened with Gwyneth, he began to pace, pausing at every pass to glance out the window to see if Gwyneth had returned.

He still couldn't decide what to do. Stay here as she had ordered and let the people of Haverleigh wonder what kind of squire didn't dare show his face to a baron, or get out of Haverleigh and never come back, as all the instincts of a thief commanded?

His heart urged him to stay. He couldn't abandon Gwyneth like that. If they could maintain the ruse a little longer, he could take his leave just as a real squire would, and the people of Haverleigh need never know the truth. After all, their ruse put her at risk, too. At best, the discovery of the truth would make her look like a foolish girl easily tricked; at worst, Gwyneth might be forced to marry at once, or be sent off to a convent. Either way, she and her father would probably lose Haverleigh. Now he could no more bear to think of that happening than she could, and as for Gwyneth's possible marriage . . .

At last there was a commotion at the gate, the sounds of a troop of soldiers arriving.

Gwyneth and DeVilliers entered the courtyard, walking in front of several mounted soldiers. DeVilliers wore a sweeping black cloak that reached to the ground, and his dark hair was brushed back from his high white forehead. Gavin was once again struck by the man's aura of power and command, and amazed that Gwyneth could walk so proud and straight behind him, as if she feared nothing in the world, and certainly not him.

Entering behind DeVilliers and Gwyneth, the baron's

men were similarly dressed in dull gray chain mail and black tunics. On their heads were helmets of plain gray metal with nose guards. They all wore swords, carried shields and looked like hardened criminals. Gavin had seen more pleasant faces on men who would steal from their own mothers.

Then he blinked and stared hard, not willing at first to believe his own eyes. Fulk, Drogo, and Bert were in the baron's cortège, and they were even riding horses.

They were not dressed like the soldiers, and Fulk looked as satisfied as if he'd just sold a fine necklace. Drogo and Bert looked less confident, but they were no less free.

He could guess what this meant, especially seeing Fulk's smug expression. They had probably come back here days ago to make sure he was dead, and instead discovered him playing Gavin of Inverlea. He didn't doubt their movements on the riverbank were what had caught his eye. Somehow they had learned that the baron would probably appreciate the news that the men of Haverleigh were learning to fight. They must have gone to the baron and offered it to him, undoubtedly for money. DeVilliers had probably brought them here to identify him and confirm their story.

Did DeVilliers guess that Gwyneth was in on the deception, or had she wisely pleaded ignorance? That would be the safest and best course. For her sake, he would gladly take the credit—or the blame—for tricking everyone, including her.

As his mind took in all he saw and the possible ramifications, he ground his fist into his palm. The truth was out, the ruse over. He was once more Gavin the thief—but he could not let Gwyneth suffer because she had tried to help her people in the only way she could think of.

He strode toward the door, fully intending to tell DeVilliers that he had fooled the young lady of Haverleigh.

As he ran down the steps, Rufus at his heels, another idea burst into his mind. What evidence did Fulk and the others have to prove that he was a thief, especially if they did not want to condemn themselves in the same breath? It was their word against that of the young man everybody in Haverleigh believed to be the squire of Sir Henry D'Argent. His word against three rogues, and if Gwyneth kept the secret . . .

Gavin entered the hall, where Moll and the other women were staring at the arriving party through the wide door leading into the courtyard.

"Excuse me," he said, pushing his way through.

As he strode into the courtyard and Rufus trotted beside him, he realized that men from the village, as well as Hollis and Emlyn and Semeli, were also arriving, their faces full of avid curiosity. They watched the dismounted soldiers with trepidation, and the baron with barely disguised loathing.

As did Gavin, for DeVilliers's hand covered Gwyneth's as if he was already claiming her for his bride.

Gwyneth saw him. Seeing her pale face, and her eyes shining with unconquerable spirit and admiration, Gavin suddenly felt invincible and capable of anything. She was worth everything—every effort, every sacrifice. If he never did another worthwhile thing in his life, he must not fail her now.

"I am delighted to see you safely returned, Lady Gwyneth," he said with the elegant drawl of a Norman nobleman. He bowed with all the grace and ease of a nobleman of the highest rank, too. "You gave us quite a start, you know, when we realized you were not at Haverleigh."

He ran a measuring gaze over the baron. "And who is this?" he asked, as if to say, "And what the devil is he doing here, the impertinent rascal?"

For a moment, Gwyneth could only stare in stunned surprise. What was Gavin doing? He was supposed to stay in his chamber, not come sauntering across the courtyard as if he were King John himself, or look at the baron as if the man smelled of something terribly unpleasant.

"Well, my lady?" Gavin inquired, raising a brow. "Are you not going to introduce me to your *friend*, who, I must say, has some very rough companions?" He looked directly at the three thieves and smiled. Slowly.

As if he was not the least bit afraid of them or what they knew about him. As if he really was . . .

Suddenly, she knew exactly what Gavin was doing.

He was going to maintain the ruse—and *why not?* It would be the word of three thieves against that of a man everybody in Haverleigh thought was Sir Henry D'Argent's squire.

She flashed Gavin a delighted, admiring smile before she turned to the baron. "My lord, allow me to present Gavin of Inverlea, squire to Sir Henry D'Argent."

"Well, well, well," DeVilliers murmured as he let go of her. His expression skeptical, he put his fists on his hips. "Tell me, how is the dear fellow?"

Gavin didn't even bat an eye. "He was well the last time I saw him."

"And when was that?"

"Six weeks ago, before I began my journey to the cathedral at Salisbury."

"He does not require your service?"

"Of course not, or I would be with him. At present, he is out of the country. On the king's business, if you *must* know." Gavin's expression became one of suspicion and injured pride. "I must say, my lord, interrogation seems a rather rude way to greet a man you have never met."

"Interrogation is the way I always begin with outlaws."

Gavin reared back as if the baron had slapped him.

"How dare you?" he demanded in outraged majesty. "How dare you imply that I, Gavin of Inverlea, son of Roger of Inverlea, descendant of kings of Scotland and the Western Isles, am outside the law?"

"Why yes, Baron," Gwyneth seconded, apparently as shocked as Gavin and the murmuring villagers. "Surely you cannot mean to accuse Gavin of Inverlea of being an outlaw?"

"I am accusing this *boy* of being an outlaw." DeVilliers smiled at Gwyneth as if she were three years old, and dim to boot. "This lad is no more the squire of Sir Henry D'Argent than I am."

A low, indignant murmur went up from the villagers. Hollis and Emlyn took a step forward, until Gavin waved them back.

"Allow me to deal with this . . . this ridiculous announcement, good people," he declared. "The poor fellow must be touched in the head."

Scowling, DeVilliers turned toward Fulk, Drogo, and Bert. "You there, come and greet your friend."

The three thieves dismounted—awkwardly—and came forward. Gavin curled his lip as if they smelled of manure.

"'Ello, Gavin," Fulk said. "Playing a little trick on the young lady, are you?"

Gavin addressed the baron as if he were a bug, and

a particularly disgusting one. "I have no idea who these people are, and I confess myself shocked—*shocked!*—that any man of intelligence would believe one word such ruffians say."

"Short memory you've got, Gavin, but then, considerin' the temptation, not so surprisin'," Fulk answered, leering at Gwyneth.

Gavin had Fulk by the throat before he could blink. "Have a care, wretch, how you speak to a lady," he said sternly. "Look again at the Lady Gwyneth as if she is a tavern wench and you will feel my blade."

Even Gwyneth felt a twinge of dread, for Gavin was the very picture of outraged nobility.

Gavin let go. Fulk stumbled, then righted himself and rubbed his throat.

Meanwhile, Gavin whirled around to face DeVilliers. "Listen here, Baron, I don't know what kind of game—"

He paused, and then, incredibly, a smile lit his face. "Is that it, my lord? This is some kind of jest? You brought them here to amuse me? I must say that while I like a good jest as well as the next man, this seems a strange way to act, considering we have never met before."

"I am not jesting," DeVilliers growled.

Gavin's eyes narrowed as he slowly crossed his arms over his chest. "Then you actually *believe* these knaves? You would believe their ludicrous story and take their word over mine? And over Lady Gwyneth's, too?"

"She is young and a girl," DeVilliers replied, glaring. "A clever rascal could easily trick her."

Gwyneth wanted to punch the baron for that. "I am not an idiot, my lord."

"No, she is not," Gavin agreed, "and that seems a strange way to talk to a young lady I understand you would like to marry. However, to keep to the business at hand and not your insults of your intended bride, what proof have these blackguards offered that I am *not* Gavin of Inverlea?"

Gwyneth saw a flicker of doubt flit across DeVilliers's face.

"I must say, my lord, when one considers the sort of person discrediting Gavin," she said, stepping forward, "it hardly seems likely that they can be telling the truth. I mean, look at them, my lord." She gestured toward the thieves. "I've heard you say more than once that you can tell a man's breeding just by looking at him. Are you really ready to believe these men over Gavin, and that he is not nobly born?"

"He ain't no more a squire than Drogo here," the scarred man snarled, his eyes burning with desperation and sweat beading his brow as he pointed at one of his companions. "Gavin's a thief, gutter born and bred."

"And if this incredible story were true, how would you know it?" Gwyneth demanded.

"We, um, we seen him in Salisbury, cutting purses."

"You did not tell someone in authority and have him arrested?"

"We had to leave."

"I'll wager you did," Gavin agreed.

"Gwyneth, this is a matter for the king's court, not you."

"My lord DeVilliers, I wouldn't waste the time of the king's judges with such a foolish charge, and neither should you. It's obvious these men are scoundrels."

"I tell ya, my lord, he's lyin'! He ain't no squire! Go ahead—test him." Fulk jerked his arm at DeVilliers's gelding. "Ask him to ride your horse."

Gwyneth could guess why Fulk had hit upon this test. Poor youths raised in the streets of towns and villages never owned any kind of a horse or had the opportunity to ride one. Gavin probably had no idea how to mount and sit in a saddle, let alone control a beast like DeVilliers's fine gelding.

"This is absurd," Gavin declared, his fists on his hips. "I won't have knaves and rascals giving me orders!"

"*I* demand it," DeVilliers said, his eyes flashing with ire. He pointed imperiously at his prancing beast. "If you are the squire of Sir Henry D'Argent, mount my horse."

Gavin lowered his arms and stared at the baron with incredulous indignation. "I will not stand here and be insulted in this fashion! Nor will I obey any orders of yours, my lord DeVilliers. I have sworn no oath of service or loyalty to you."

DeVilliers smiled, a cold, cruel smile that filled Gwyneth with fear. "No man speaks to me like that and goes unchallenged. And it is more than impertinence for you to train an armed force against me, boy."

"Is that what all this is about?" Gavin scoffed. "I was merely showing a few fellows some tricks that might come in useful someday if they ever find themselves attacked by brigands on the road, as I was. And for that you insult my honor?"

"Who said they were being trained to fight against *you*, my lord?" Gwyneth demanded. "Even if I were having my men trained, it would be only to protect Haverleigh against unlawful invaders, and there is nothing wrong with that. Or do you include yourself in that description?"

"You are nothing more than impertinent children, the pair of you!" DeVilliers cried, shaking his fist with rage. "Do you think you and your men could ever be any match for a real fighting force? If so, that shows what fools you are!"

Gwyneth lifted her chin. "My lord, now you would insult every man here?"

A low rumble of discontent rose from the crowd.

DeVilliers threw out his chest. "If they think they

are a match for my men, they are indeed fools. Would you care to put the matter to a test? A *hastilude*, your men against mine, will prove if farmers can ever have any hope of success against professional soldiers."

Despite her pride in her men and belief that Gavin had taught them well, Gwyneth felt panic rising. DeVilliers was proposing a form of competition that was not a civilized affair, but two groups of men clashing in a mélée, a free-for-all with few rules. Although no one was supposed to die in a such a meeting, given the nature of the mélée, men sometimes did, or were seriously injured.

"If you do not accept this challenge, I ride at once for the king and tell him that a base impostor has tricked his way into the household of Haverleigh, and that the foolish young lady of Haverleigh has let him train a fighting force to use against her neighbor."

"This is ridiculous!" Gwyneth protested, not waiting for Gavin to respond. "Both your charge and your proposal. For one thing, foot soldiers do not participate in the *hastilude*."

"Then let us not call this by its formal name, my lady," DeVilliers replied. "Let us call it a test. If Gavin and your men do not wish to face mine because they fear failure—"

"Never!" Fenwick called out. "We're ready!"

Others in the crowd, including Hollis and Emlyn, shouted their agreement, and other things besides.

"Well, my lady, it seems your men feel up to the challenge," DeVilliers said as he smiled his horrible smile. "What about you, Gavin of the gutters? Are you prepared to lead them against my men on the field?"

Gavin nodded once. "Yes."

A cheer went up from the villagers, which drowned out the mercenaries' jeering.

In the ensuing cacophony, DeVilliers faced Gwyneth and spoke so that only she could hear. "At best that boy is a liar and a rogue and you are a silly child to believe him. If you know what he is and think to trick me, you are worse than a fool. Do you really believe farmers and peasants can beat battle-hardened mercenaries from all over Europe? I am going to have Haverleigh, and you, and there is *nothing* you or this boy or these bumpkins can do to stop me."

Gwyneth's stomach knotted to hear his words and see the fierce determination and hatred in his eyes. It would be better to die than to become the wife of a man who looked at her thus.

And who smiled to see her dismay.

As the cheering subsided, the baron turned once more to Gavin. "I do not have my armor, and I'm sure your men could use the extra time to practice, useless though it will be, so I propose we meet in the river meadow tomorrow, just after midday."

Gavin tore his gaze from Gwyneth's pale face,

wondering what DeVilliers had whispered to her to make her look so stricken. He bowed again. "As you wish, my lord. I look forward to it."

DeVilliers nodded, spun on his heel, and strode to his horse. He barked an order to his men, and they rode out of Haverleigh.

Only the jingle of their bridles, the squeak of their saddles, and the sound of their horses' hooves on the cobblestones broke the silence until they were out of the gate.

CHAPTER EIGHTEEN

As if a dam had burst, everybody started talking at once.

Ignoring the noise, Gavin hurried to Gwyneth. "What did he say to you, there at the end? You look like you're about to swoon."

He put his arms around her and the crowd parted to let them through as he led her to the hall. She saw Semeli's worried face, and Hollis's, as well as those of all the others, but she didn't speak. She just let herself be helped, held safe for a moment in Gavin's strong arms.

When they entered the hall, she whispered, "Let's go to the solar, where we can speak in private."

He nodded, and arm in arm they went through the hall past the servants gathered there.

Once in the solar, Gwyneth sat on the wide stone windowsill. Gavin stood before her, concerned and anxious, while Rufus laid his head in her lap and looked at her as if he feared for her, too.

Gwyneth knew what must be done, because DeVilliers was right. They, all of them—Gavin, her tenants, her—were no match for the soldiers DeVilliers had hired, or him, either. She should have guessed that her continual refusal of his "assistance" and his offer to marry him would make him do something like this. He was ambitious, vicious, and cruel, and she had been a desperate fool, blinded by ridiculous hopes.

There was but one thing to do now: admit that, or Gavin and her people would pay for her mistake, possibly with their lives.

"Gavin, you must go at once," she said, trying to sound firm, but not quite managing it. "My men must not meet the baron's mercenaries on the field. Against his other troops, Fenwick and the others would have had a chance, thanks to you—at least enough that DeVilliers would have had to think twice before he threatened us. But against these new men? Too many will be hurt or killed."

Gavin reached out, took her slender hands in his, and gazed at her upturned face. "He's frightened you, I know, but—"

"If I am frightened of DeVilliers, it's because I should be," she said as she pulled her hands from his. "My soldiers are only farmers who have had a few lessons in how to wield a sword."

Gavin's grave brown eyes searched her face. "Have you so little faith in me, or your men? Do you think that they will go easily to defeat, or that we're cowards?"

"It isn't whether you and the others are brave enough, Gavin." She rose and regarded him steadily, willing him to see that she spoke the truth. "DeVilliers has outmaneuvered me by hiring those mercenaries. He has defeated us even before we took the field."

"Your men are not afraid, and neither am I. We will show DeVilliers and his men what we can do."

He sounded so convinced, so sure of himself. "Even at the risk of their lives?"

"If it gets too rough, we'll surrender. But give us a chance, Gwyneth. Don't ask us to give up before we've tried."

"Gavin," she said, and now her voice was steady, because she was determined to do what she thought was right, "you're only a poor boy who can protect himself against ruffians, and while you have done a fine job training the others, it cannot be enough, not against those mercenaries."

Gavin's heart seemed to fall to his feet. She was so certain that he and the others would be defeated. "Your men are good, better than I ever thought they could be."

Her expression softened and her eyes filled with a sorrow that it pained him to see. "It isn't only of my men that I'm thinking. You must leave right away. It's too dangerous for you to stay."

"I am not afraid of DeVilliers," he replied, meaning it. He would face more than the baron if her freedom was at stake. "It is only Fulk's word against mine that I am not a squire."

"For now, but for how long can we maintain the ruse?"

He gently took hold of her shoulders as he tried to make her understand why he would not—could not— leave, at least not yet. "I haven't forgotten that I am only a thief. I have never been anything else until here, for a time, I was more than that. I was worthy to teach your men how to fight. I was worthy of their admiration and respect. I was worthy enough for your kiss. That is not something I will easily give up.

"As for DeVilliers and his men, I have spent my whole life running away. From those who would hurt me, from those I robbed, from those who would punish me. I have tasted freedom here, Gwyneth, and more. These men respect me. I will not flee like a cowardly outlaw, and you must not ask them to surrender without trying."

"Gavin, please, you must leave Haverleigh." Tears filled her eyes and her lips began to tremble, the sight of her sorrow tearing at his heart. "It's too dangerous for you. If anything were to happen to you, I couldn't bear it."

His grip on her shoulders loosened as he studied her sorrowful eyes, seeing worry, despair . . . and something more, something he had never seen in anybody's eyes as they looked at him, not since his mother had taken her life.

Love.

He knew it, in the core of his soul, to the bottom of his heart. Gwyneth was asking him to go because she loved him, and her love made her fear for him.

"Oh, Gwyneth," he whispered as he gathered her into

a gentle embrace, more determined than ever to stay and prove himself. "Gwyneth, don't you see? If I go now, a poor, worthless thief is all I will ever be. Even if I die, I would rather die as Gavin of Inverlea than Gavin the thief." He drew back and raised her trembling chin with his knuckle. "We mustn't give up yet. Believe this, men who have trained to fight in one way can be confused by the unexpected. That is where we will have the advantage. Please, give me this chance, Gwyneth, to prove myself not just to DeVilliers, but to you. And your men deserve the chance to defend their honor, too."

Loving her with all his heart, he leaned close and pressed a gentle kiss on her lips.

She clung to him. "Oh, Gavin, you need not do this for my sake."

He caressed her cheek. "I want to. I want to prove that I am worthy of your faith in me."

"You already have."

Someone cleared his throat.

They jumped apart and Gavin flushed with embarrassment as Fenwick entered, followed by Hollis—holding Semeli's hand—as well as Emlyn and what appeared to be the whole troop of men he had trained.

"My lady," Fenwick said, "forgive us burstin' in on you like this, but me and the lads here was worried you was trying to talk our Gavin out of letting us show them louts what good men are made of. We'll give DeVilliers and his men a hiding they won't soon forget. And as for our Gavin, he can take that black crow of a baron any day o' the week. Right, lads?"

A rousing cheer went up, seeming to rattle the very stones of the solar.

Gavin's chest nearly burst with pride at their confidence in him, and a grin blossomed at their confirmation of what he had told Gwyneth.

"And as for bein' an outlaw, Gavin, we knew you wasn't no squire the first time you opened your mouth."

Shocked and stunned, Gavin almost fell over. A quick glance at Gwyneth showed that she was just as dumbfounded.

"Scot or not, you didn't sound like no squire we ever heard. No, nor act like one, neither, as we menfolk realized right quick." He shoved Hollis on the shoulder. "Them young ones took longer."

"You've known all along?" Gavin murmured incredulously.

Gwyneth took a tentative step toward Semeli. "And you . . . ?"

Her friend nodded.

Gwyneth rushed to embrace Semeli. "I hated not being able to tell you, but I thought it was dangerous for you to know."

Semeli hugged her back, and there were tears in the regal girl's black eyes. "Of course I knew that. And my heart ached to tell you that you did not have to keep your secret, but I knew you would worry more, so I did not."

Gavin cleared his throat as the men shuffled awkwardly. "So, even you knew, Hollis?" he asked as the girls stepped apart. "Why didn't you say anything?"

"We was afraid you might bolt if we did," Hollis said with a roguish grin. "We didn't want you to run off before we learned what you had to teach."

"Does *everybody* know?" Gwyneth asked. "Does Thomas?"

"Oh, no. Too stupid to figure it out, that one, and we wasn't goin' t' tell him," Fenwick replied. "He'd go runnin' off to DeVilliers quick as a wink if he did. Seems he's been runnin' off to DeVilliers a fair amount as it is, ain't that right, Hollis?"

Hollis traced the outline of a stone in the floor with his toe. "I'm sorry to say, it is," he admitted as he looked at them from under his brow. "I wasn't sure, so the last time he left home, I followed him a ways and he was making straight for the baron's castle. I told Semeli about it this morning. She was going to tell you tonight."

Semeli nodded her head. "That is true."

"Listen, Gavin," Fenwick said, "we don't give a toss where you was born or who your parents were. You're as fine as any nobleman to us, and always will be."

The men nodded their agreement.

"When this is over, if you want to come and be a soldier with me, I'd be pleased and proud to have your company," Hollis added.

Gavin went to Hollis and grasped his hand. "I'll be pleased and proud to join you."

When he had to leave Gwyneth, it might hurt less to be traveling with a friend, and to honest employment.

It might.

"Here now, let us through!" Peg cried from the back of the crowd. "Make way for the earl."

Her eyes wide with surprise, Gwyneth stared with eyes as big as cart wheels as her father entered the room, leaning on Peg's arm for support.

"What is this, a riot?" the earl demanded genially.

Gavin recognized the man he had seen lying on the bed that first night. There was color in his cheeks now, although not nearly so much as there was in Gwyneth's as she looked at him in awe. "Father! What are you doing here?"

"Couldn't sleep with all that racket in the courtyard, could I?" Then he smiled and held out his arms, and Gwyneth ran into his embrace.

Her joy seemed to spread out and encompass Gavin, too, as if the earl were the father he had never known.

After hugging Lord William, Gwyneth drew back, wiping her eyes. "I am so happy!"

"Yes, well, I am happy to be out of my bedchamber,

too," the earl said, his own eyes suspiciously moist and his voice thick with emotion. Then he cleared his throat. "If everyone but Fenwick and this young man who has been training my tenants—and very well, too, Peg tells me— will please leave the room, we have strategy to discuss for tomorrow."

"Father, you know . . . ?"

Lord William smiled tenderly at his daughter. "My dear, there is nothing that happens at Haverleigh that I do not hear about eventually. Why do you think I asked for Peg so often, eh? She knows everything, and tells it, too."

"Only to you, my lord!" Peg cried, obviously offended.

"How long have you known about the training? And Gavin?" Gwyneth asked her father.

"Since it began. Remember this, little girl of mine— it's very difficult to keep a secret in a castle. Now, go with Semeli and prepare a feast, or as much as you can manage on one boar."

"You heard about that, too?"

"It seems Etienne cannot keep a secret, either." He eyed Gavin, who flushed beneath his scrutiny. "Peg was right. Thief or not, you are a very fine-looking young man. I could believe you are a squire myself. But to name Sir Henry . . . perhaps not the best choice."

"My lord, I—" Gavin began apologetically.

The earl waved his hand dismissively. "If Gwyneth had such faith in you, so will I, and we will not call you a thief again—unless you steal something from me." He smiled at Gwyneth again and gestured at the door. "Now, leave us, my child, and let the men plan their strategy."

"*Mon Dieu*, whoever would have thought even *I* could create a feast with one boar!" Etienne cried with happy triumph as he put the last of the steaming meat pasties on the work table.

"If there was a cook in England who could do it, Etienne, I knew it would be you," Gwyneth replied with a smile as she cut up a thick loaf of bread. She had been helping as best she could to keep her mind from what was happening in the solar, with very little effect. All she could think about was Gavin, her father, and Fenwick planning and plotting to defeat the baron and his mercenaries tomorrow.

Peg arrived from the hall where she had been supervising the setting up of the tables. She sniffed the delicious aromas. "We're ready, my lady."

"Excellent. A few more moments for my stew and it will be perfection!" Etienne declared, kissing his fingertips with a hearty smack.

"Good. I'll tell the serving maids to come."

Etienne nodded and bustled off to stir the large pot on the hearth.

"My lady, you'd best go to the hall," Peg suggested.

"I will," she replied, heading for the corridor. She wondered if she had time to wash her face and tidy her hair before the meal began.

"You are looking very serious."

She started and looked up to discover Gavin standing right in front of her, a smile on his face.

He backed her into the corridor, where they would not be seen from the hall or the kitchen.

"You're not going to suggest I leave again, are you?" he asked, his low voice sending thrilling little ripples of excitement through her. "Because I won't. At least, not yet."

He put his arms around her and she slipped hers about his waist. "No, I was not planning to ask you to leave again."

His lips were barely inches from her mouth. "Good."

He kissed her gently, wonderfully. Her heartbeat quickened, her blood throbbed, and her heart fairly sang with the joy of her love for him.

But he did not kiss her long before he stopped and looked around as if searching for spies. "I suppose I shouldn't do that." *

She didn't like the finality of his tone. "Not here, anyway."

"Why, my lady!" he cried, his voice astonished but his eyes dancing with merriment, "I knew you were bold, but

Moll could scarcely be more brazen."

She decided to be truly bold and ask the question that had been troubling her. "When the contest is over and you have proved yourself to be Gavin of Inverlea, what will you do?"

His eyes darkened with emotion as he looked into hers. "I never thought of my future before I came here, beyond staying alive. Then I met you. Shall I tell you what I aim for now, Lady Gwyneth of Haverleigh?"

She could scarcely draw breath as she nodded her agreement.

"I dream of becoming worthy of your hand some day."

"Oh, Gavin," she murmured, leaning her head against his chest, "you are more than worthy of it now."

She felt him shake his head. "Not yet. But I have heard of soldiers who were knighted by their lords and even given estates. Some go on to win prizes and honors at tournaments. If it is possible to achieve a knighthood and an estate and wealth through hard work and determination, Gwyneth, I'll do it. For you."

Sadness warred with the happiness his love created, but she blinked back her tears. "That means you'll have to leave Haverleigh."

"For a time."

"I would marry you if you were a blacksmith or a carpenter, Gavin."

"Perhaps you would, but to rob you of your status . . . that would be the worst thing I could ever steal."

"If you go, you might be hurt, or killed."

"I'll risk it. And I'll be honest with you, Gwyneth. I like the respect I've had here, and I do not want to lose that, either." His gaze intensified. "Can you understand that? Will you wait for me?"

"Yes, Gavin, my love." She raised herself on her toes and kissed him, promising without words that she had faith in him.

CHAPTER NINETEEN

"My lady!" Peg stood in the door leading into the hall, her hands on her hips and fire in her eyes.

"This is no proper behavior for a lady!" she cried, aghast. "What would your sainted mother say?"

They drew apart, but Gwyneth kept hold of Gavin's hand in defiance of the woman's indignation. She would defy far more than Peg for him. "We were talking."

"I was young myself once, so you're not fooling me with that," Peg noted sternly, but even as she spoke, her fiery gaze softened. "Aye, young and in love, so I'll say nothing of this to your father."

In view of what Gwyneth had heard today, she had her doubts about that.

"I can keep quiet if it's a little kissing in the corridor," Peg declared. "Not that your father would be able to say much against that. Why, I remember the time your mother and him was found in the barn over a month before they wed."

This was one story Gwyneth had never heard Peg tell before, and she listened with unabashed fascination.

"Straw in their hair and their clothes so rumpled I

thought I'd never get the wrinkles——" Peg's eyes widened a moment as if she suddenly realized there was a reason she had never told Gwyneth this story. "But enough about that. Come and see your father in his place once more."

They followed her, and as they entered the hall, pride and joy filled Gwyneth to see her father again sitting at the high table on the dais of the great hall of Haverleigh, overlooking the men who would try to win him honor tomorrow.

She squeezed Gavin's hand, her heart almost full to bursting.

It would have been, if Gavin could stay.

Her father spotted them and gestured for them to join him on the dais. Rufus, who had been sitting behind her father's chair, took his usual place at her side. Semeli was sitting with Hollis, and Emlyn was nearby, demonstrating to Fenwick yet again, apparently, the proper way to draw a bow.

"Gwyneth, you sit on my left," her father said, "and Gavin—who has a most impressive grasp of battle for one so young—may sit on my right."

Gwyneth fairly beamed. That was a place of great honor and told her that her father did indeed think very highly of Gavin.

After Father Bernard said the grace and the meal began, it was almost like old times. Familiar voices filled the hall, full of suppressed excitement. Moll moved among the tables, hips swaying as always—but she never once looked at the high table, or Gavin. She did, however, linger rather long at Darton's table, and giggled at everything he said.

The same it was, yet very different, too. One glance at Gavin reminded her of what had changed. How *she* had changed.

The women began to serve the bread and ale, and as they did, Gwyneth realized her father was telling Gavin about lords he knew, men he thought would be good masters. Gavin must have told him his plans to become a soldier. Had he told her father everything, about wanting a knighthood, and her?

As she tried to figure out how she could ask him, Thomas strode into the hall and came to a flabbergasted halt.

"Greetings, Thomas!" her father called out. His voice was far from robust, but it was loud enough to carry over the noise.

"My lord!" Thomas gasped. "You're . . . you're better?"

The earl gestured for Thomas to approach. The reeve obeyed, passing the men and women who regarded him with distinctly unfriendly eyes. "You sound disappointed, Thomas."

"Disappointed? No, my lord, not at all. I'm delighted

to see you so well. I'm simply surprised, that's all. I had no idea—"

"Did my daughter not inform you that James said I was recovering?"

Gwyneth watched Thomas squirm. It was not pleasant, but he had made her squirm for weeks. Let him know what it was like, so he would think twice before he upset anyone else. "Yes, my lord, she did, but I did not dare to be hopeful."

"Why not?"

She glanced at Gavin, who leaned back in his chair, a little smile on his face, as if he were enjoying this, too. As for Hollis, his eyes were as bright with glee as sunshine in the summer.

"I dared not hope because . . . because your fate was in the hand of God." Thomas smiled as if he believed God Himself had brought that excuse to his lips.

"Exactly. And God has seen fit to save me. Tell me, how fares my neighbor, the Baron DeVilliers?"

Thomas seemed to shrink. "The baron, my lord?"

"Yes. You have just been to Aldenborough, although I must say it seems odd to go that far east when Salisbury lies to the west. I gather you have been a frequent guest of the baron's of late."

Her father got to his feet and leaned heavily upon the table. "You have been seen, Thomas. What business did my reeve have with my neighbor—my neighbor who covets my estate and my daughter, too—that made those frequent journeys necessary?"

"My lord, I . . . I was telling him how you were."

Gwyneth had rarely seen her father enraged, but this was one such time as he glared at Thomas trembling before him. "I wonder, then, Thomas, that you did not tell us about the soldiers he was hiring—hulking brutes, the lot of them. I could tell that from my chamber window. You must have seen them. Hulking brutes are hard to hide."

"My lord, I did not think they would be used against you."

"Don't treat me as if I were a fool, Thomas. We both know otherwise. You are a traitor to your lord, and you will leave Haverleigh at once. If you do not, I will have you arrested for betraying your trust as reeve of Haverleigh. Do you understand me?"

"But my lord, I was only thinking of your daughter. She couldn't hold Haverleigh by herself, not with you being so sick. We needed a man—"

"We needed a loyal reeve who would help her, not criticize her every move! It is to her credit that she did as well as she did, regardless of your interference. Now, go, and never come back to Haverleigh again, or you will be sorry."

At the earl's harsh command, Thomas scurried away as if he were a mouse fleeing a burning barn.

There was a moment of silence.

Then Emlyn jumped to his feet and raised his mug of ale. "Here's to a good riddance. Aye, and here's to our lord and to his daughter, too!"

The earl smiled, then raised his ale. "And here's to Gavin of Haverleigh, who shall lead you all to victory tomorrow!"

Unable to sleep, Gavin watched the sun rise the next morning. The indigo sky lightened, followed by brilliant pink and orange tinting its blue depths. It was going to be a fine day, one that could have been made for a fair or festival—or a battle.

Sighing, he turned from the window and surveyed the now familiar chamber. He thought back to his first day here, when he had awakened confused and afraid, before Gwyneth had come with her determined eyes and incredible plan.

Yet she had done more than turn the farmers and peasants of Haverleigh into a fighting force. She had turned him into something he would not have believed possible: an honest, respectable young man with a goal.

The door started to open and Rufus appeared, bringing a grin to Gavin's face. "Are you my rooster, Rufus?"

"You are awake?"

He looked up to see Gwyneth cautiously entering the chamber. She wore a simple gown of plain blue, with an equally unembellished leather belt around her waist, and her hair was drawn back into two braids without adornment. She carried something long and wrapped in linen in her hands.

Despite her austere attire, no princess in Christendom could ever look more lovely to him.

"You should not be here," he noted reluctantly as she set her bundle down on his cot.

After Peg's interruption yesterday, he realized he had better behave with more decorum, as difficult as it might be, if he was to have any chance of ever being considered worthy of aspiring to Gwyneth's hand.

His love gave him a winsome smile. "You may have learned your role of chivalrous squire too well. However, I have something important to give you. And . . ."

"And?" he prompted, delighted by her charming blush far more than by the prospect of any present, unless it be another kiss.

"And I wanted a little time alone with you."

He held open his arms and she hurried into them.

"I know it is the practice of ladies to give their chosen champions favors," he said, toying with one of her braids and nodding at the gift a little while later as they sat on the cot, no longer kissing, "but that looks a little large and heavy to be a scarf."

She lifted it onto her lap and began to undo the wrappings. "I'll gladly give you a scarf to wear, too."

She revealed a sword in a scabbard of wonderfully worked leather. A red jewel in the hilt of the weapon gleamed in the early-morning sunlight as she held it out to him. "This was my brother's tournament sword. I want you to wear it today."

"Oh, by the saints, Gwyneth," he breathed, over-whelmed by her offer. He took the weapon in his hands, appreciating the value of it, and the trust that she would let him, a thief, even hold it.

Touched as he was, he couldn't help asking, "What will your father say?"

"I suggested this to him last night, when Emlyn was asking you if you would station him on the battlements with his bow in case there was foul play."

"Ah, yes, he is very keen to wound anybody getting too rough," Gavin said with a chuckle.

"My father agreed that you should wear this, so you will, won't you?"

Gavin rose and humbly knelt before her, as if she were a queen seated on a throne. "I would be honored, my lady, although I will admit I would be more honored to wear your scarf."

She smiled very prettily, and he couldn't resist the urge to lean forward and kiss her again.

"Peg was right," Semeli remarked from the doorway. "We should have set a watch outside your door."

"Would you have liked me to set a watch on you and Hollis last night?" Gwyneth countered even as her cheeks reddened. "You were a long time in the buttery together, fetching that ale."

"A princess of Persia may stay as long as she likes in the buttery," Semeli retorted as she came into the room. She had a scarlet bundle of cloth in her hands. "And you should ask me about Moll. She still hasn't come to the kitchen. Peg says she must have spent all night with the smith's son because of the way she was looking at him in the hall."

Gavin and Gwyneth exchanged smiles.

"What's that?" Gwyneth asked, nodding at Semeli's bundle.

"Your father has sent this for Gavin, because today he represents Haverleigh." She held up a woolen surcoat, the long tunic a knight wore over his armor. Embroidered on it was a golden lion, crouched as if to strike.

"That was my brother's, too," Gwyneth whispered in explanation, and he saw the glimmer of tears in her eyes.

He took it and held it reverently. Thankfully. Feeling as if he didn't deserve half the honors they were giving him. "I . . . I'm not worthy to wear it."

"The earl thinks you are," Semeli declared, breaking the emotional spell woven around them. "He also says you are to wear the armor that goes with it, so it does not matter what you think. Now I am to summon you to mass. Considering the bumps and bruises likely to come, a few prayers for God's protection would be a good idea."

She marched to the door, then stood and waited for them to follow her. Gwyneth took Gavin's hand, her slender fingers wrapping about his, warm and strong, and together they left the chamber.

Shortly after midday, when the sun was high in the sky, the two forces faced each other across the river meadow. Nearest the river were the baron and his mercenaries. Near the road, Gavin and his men waited, nervous but unafraid.

Wearing a black surcoat with a silver dragon rampant, his chain mail gleaming dully beneath it, the baron sat on his black war-horse. His soldiers were on foot, their long shields resting on the ground as they relaxed and joked, obviously no more concerned about their opposition than if the earl of Haverleigh was sending a gaggle of geese against them.

Gavin's men had swords and shields from the Haverleigh armory, and none of them was mounted. As Fulk had said, Gavin could not ride, so he would rather be on foot than precariously seated on a horse he could barely control.

Facing the field, the earl sat upon a bench, Gwyneth beside him. Behind them stood the people of Haverleigh and the servants of the castle, Semeli at the front. Rufus sat near Gwyneth, his haunches quivering as if he felt the tension in the air.

The baron rode forward and addressed the earl. "We shall await your signal to begin," he called out as if this were a great privilege he was bestowing, although it was the earl's right to give the signal because this was his land.

Gwyneth got to her feet and came toward Gavin, a pale blue scarf in her hands. With DeVilliers watching, she tied it about Gavin's upper arm. "You will best him."

"For your sake, I'll try."

She nodded, and raised herself on her toes to kiss his cheek. "Good luck, my champion."

His throat tightened as she went back to join her father. For her sake, and to show her that her faith in him was justified, he would fight as he had never fought before.

The earl raised his hand. The men all held their breath.

When Lord William abruptly lowered his arm, they charged.

CHAPTER TWENTY

The two groups met with a great roar and clash of sword on shield. Some fell and Gavin knew a few were injured, but he kept his gaze firmly fastened on DeVilliers. The baron rode straight for him, his sword raised and his face contorted with rage.

Gavin planted his feet, Rylan's tournament sword held low and loose in his right hand, the shield on his left arm covering his chest. As he waited, he summoned every ounce of patience and strength and courage he possessed, until the baron's horse was almost upon him. Then, lashing out with his sword as if it were a snake, he jumped out of the way.

Gavin's blow did not penetrate the mail on DeVilliers's leg, but it did catch and tear a gash in his surcoat.

The baron wheeled his horse. "That cost more than your life is worth," he snarled, his voice loud over the sound of the men fighting nearby.

Again the baron charged, and Gavin stood as before— but this time as the baron went to strike, Gavin threw down his sword, ducked the blow, and reached for the baron's outstretched arm. DeVilliers gave a roar of dismay as Gavin hauled him from his horse, and he hit the ground heavily.

Gavin's shield was broken and he shrugged it off. He quickly retrieved his sword, but by the time he had it in his hands again, DeVilliers had struggled to his feet. The baron gripped the hilt of his long broadsword with both hands.

"I swear you're going to die, you damned rogue!" DeVilliers cried as he came closer.

Gavin didn't answer. He would need all his energy to beat the baron. He would not waste it with talk.

The baron started to circle around him. "You think you stand a chance against me, thief? With that *toy*? You're an even greater fool than I thought. I will kill you, and then I'll move against the earl. Every noble in England will agree that the earl is not in his right mind when I tell them about you. King John certainly will."

Gavin, feinting, ducked left. As the baron followed his motion, he quickly moved the other way. If he could get the baron's sword away from him . . .

The baron was fast and parried the blow. "Tricky, are you? That won't be enough. I had a good teacher, thief. Who was yours? That scarred blackguard I hanged yesterday, along with his fellows?"

Gavin commanded himself to ignore any thought that did not have to do with fighting the baron. He had used distraction too often not to see it for the weapon it was.

"Aren't you going to ask me why I did that? What charge I made against them?"

"I can guess," Gavin hissed, his gaze focused on the baron's weapon.

"I hanged them because it pleased me to. Imagine, then, the delight I will have when I kill you. Slowly." The baron laughed, but all his talking had robbed him of some breath.

Holding his sword in front of him, Gavin lowered it so that the tip was almost in the dirt, leaving his chest exposed. Crouching more, he began to sway from side to side.

"Getting tired, are you, thief?" the baron jeered as he advanced, his right foot forward. "Obviously, such sport is not for knaves. It is for a trained knight like me."

DeVilliers raised his sword, the blade over his right shoulder. As he did, Gavin lunged and brought his sword upward with all his strength.

The baron cried out and staggered back, blood dripping from the tear in the mail covering his forearm.

"By God, you're going to pay for that, thief," DeVilliers growled. He advanced on Gavin again, weapon raised, yet wavering, his arm weakened by the wound.

"Stop in the name of the king! Lower your weapons!"

At the cry of the unfamiliar yet imperious voice, Gavin risked a glance at the source. A tall, finely attired knight stood beside Gwyneth and her father. A troop of mounted soldiers had joined the people watching, and four of them held pennants bearing the coat of arms of the king of England.

Around them on the field, the combatants took heed of the command and those who were still standing lowered their swords. With relief, Gavin saw that his friends were bloodied and battered, but most of them were on their feet. The baron's mercenaries, however, were either flat on their backs, hunched over in pain or . . . gone.

Triumph and pride surged through him. They had won.

And then the flash of metal caught his eye as the baron ignored the command and lifted his sword again. Gavin twisted, barely getting his sword up in time to block the blow. With both hands, he swung his weapon, catching the baron's and wrenching it from his grasp. It flew through the air and landed near Gavin's discarded shield.

The baron dived for it. Gavin followed him, cautious and determined.

"Enough!"

Gavin hesitated and looked over his shoulder. The man he had seen standing with Gwyneth and the earl strode toward them, his expression fierce and majestic. He could believe this man represented the king and so, keeping a watch on the baron out of the corner of his eye, he lowered his sword. His enemy staggered to his feet, his arm bloody, his surcoat torn and grass stained.

The man came to stand between them. He was indeed tall and broad shouldered, his chest wide and his legs long and lean. His brown hair was cut in the Norman fashion, as if a bowl had been put on his head, but he looked better than most who sported that style, perhaps because of his sharp cheekbones and strong jaw.

The stranger ran a swift, measuring gaze over Gavin, then faced DeVilliers. "Well, Desmond, we meet again."

"Sir Henry," the baron said, trying to catch his breath. He looked past the man to Gavin, and there was a gleam of malicious glee in his eyes. "I was told you were out of the country."

Was this Sir Henry D'Argent?

Gavin suddenly felt sick.

"I have been back at court only a fortnight. I was on my way to collect my squire when I thought to call upon my old friend, the earl of Haverleigh. Imagine my surprise upon learning that young Gavin was here—and fighting you." Sir Henry smiled with his lips, but not his eyes. "And I do believe he was winning."

As if the surprising revelation of the identity of the stranger was not enough to take years off Gavin's life, Sir Henry clapped a hand on his shoulder, smiled at him as if they were old friends, and nodded at Gwyneth, who hurried to stand beside him. "I can see why you lingered here. She's very pretty. But you should have let me know where you were."

Gavin would have sat down if there had been anything to sit on other than the grass.

"What kind of game is this?" DeVilliers snarled, coming toward them and still clutching his sword. "He's no more your squire than I am, D'Argent, and you know it!"

Sir Henry's hand went to the hilt of his sword. "Soon enough you will wish you *were* a squire, DeVilliers. You've been beaten, and I have to tell you, in more than this." He raised his voice and called to the troops carrying the king's flag. "Arrest him, by order of King John."

"*What?*" The color drained from DeVilliers's face.

"You gambled once too often on the king's friendship," Sir Henry replied as his men surrounded DeVilliers. "We have a suspicious king who sees conspiracies everywhere, and one who, like his brother, is forever in need of funds. A wise man would have paid his taxes and taken care not to create suspicion about his ambitions, but you are not wise, Desmond, and you have failed on both counts.

"I'm sure I need not tell you how the king feels about nobles who do not pay all the tax they should," Sir Henry continued, "while also hiring expensive mercenaries who have no loyalty save to the man who pays them."

Like a cornered animal, DeVilliers spun around and saw that he was indeed alone.

"As if that weren't bad enough—and I assure you, it is," Sir Henry went on in that same calm, inexorable, unforgiving tone, "he also heard of your impatience to marry this young lady, and of course he knew the earl was unwell. The estate of Haverleigh would make you even richer, and better able to hire more mercenaries, while you still owe much to the Crown. It is not a pleasant situation for a king to contemplate, Desmond."

"I am a loyal subject of His Majesty!" DeVilliers cried, backing away. He took a deep breath and straightened, a vestige of his former haughty manner coming to his face. "It is no crime to marry a neighbor's daughter. Nor is it a crime to hire soldiers. As for the taxes, naturally I have every intention of paying the full amount as soon as the harvest is completed."

His eyes full of mocking skepticism, Sir Henry smiled. "Naturally."

"It is no secret that our harvest last year was not as good as in past years. Even the lady of Haverleigh cannot dispute that," DeVilliers countered. "And does John not take it amiss that the earl's daughter seeks to train her people to fight? They might rebel against their overlord, and the king."

The smile disappeared from Sir Henry's face, to be replaced by outright scorn. "You seem to forget, no lord of Haverleigh has ever betrayed the Crown, or a man's trust." His eyes glinted with a hardness that made Gavin flinch. "Unlike you and your family, Desmond. The DeVillierses have always been a nest of vipers waiting to strike."

His face red, his eyes like the boar in its death throes, DeVilliers shook his fist at Sir Henry. "You and John can both go to hell! I have done nothing I was not within my rights to do!"

"So you may explain to the king and his court when you are brought before them. For now, it is merely my task to have you taken to Westminster to face them. Oh, and to take control of your estate. Whether you are guilty of treason or not, John has stripped you of Aldenborough for having failed to pay your taxes."

Sir Henry gestured to his men. "Bind him and take him to the castle. We start for Westminster at dawn tomorrow."

The furious vitality drained from DeVilliers's face as the king's men did as Sir Henry had ordered. Kicking and screaming like a child having a tantrum, Baron DeVilliers was ignominiously dragged from the field.

Their enemy charged with treason, his estate forfeited, Sir Henry acting as if Gavin really was his squire—what other astonishing, wonderful things could possibly happen today? Gavin wondered.

As DeVilliers's curses and protestations of innocence diminished in the distance, Sir Henry turned toward Gavin. He smiled, but his gaze was shrewd and searching. "So, you would try to pass yourself off as my squire, eh?"

Gavin flushed. "Sir, it was all my idea, so if anyone is to be punished—"

Gwyneth squeezed his hand. "It's all right, Gavin. He's not angry."

"Not exactly," the nobleman corrected. "I would have been, if you were a poor swordsman. However, although you are rough and unschooled, given the proper training, you would no doubt make a formidable opponent. I'm sure DeVilliers learned that lesson. Besides, it was worth claiming you as my squire to see the look on that black-guard's face.

"Now, let us all go to the hall. I want the whole story, not just the bits the earl had time to tell me while a group of peasants defeated the most ferocious band of mercenaries in England."

Later, as they sat together in the solar on chairs the servants had hastened to bring, Sir Henry shook his head with disbelief. "It seems an incredible story. And you concocted this plan all on your own, my lady?"

"I was desperate, sir," Gwyneth said by way of explan-ation. Gavin sat beside her, and they faced Sir Henry and her father. Below, they could hear the sounds of merry-making. The celebrating promised to continue well into the night, but Gwyneth did not begrudge her people the celebration; the men especially deserved it.

Her father smiled at her indulgently. "My daughter is prone to flights of fancy and amazing schemes. However, I must confess, this is beyond anything she has ever done before."

"And you, young scalawag," Sir Henry said to Gavin,

"what made you think you could pull it off?"

Gavin slid a glance at Gwyneth. "Lady Gwyneth's faith in me."

"Well, you certainly could have fooled me on the field," Sir Henry said. "Although your fighting style is unique, I took you for a nobleman, born and bred." He ran his hand over his chin as he regarded Gavin thoughtfully. "And now you plan to become a soldier?"

"Yes, sir."

"Is that all?"

Gwyneth's breath caught in her throat as she wondered if Gavin would reveal their *other* hopeful plans. "No, sir. I would become a knight, if I could."

"Ah."

"I know it will take time and much effort, but I am willing to work hard and do my best to make it happen."

Sir Henry drummed his fingers on the arm of his chair a moment, then turned to the earl. "You're a good judge of character, William. What say you? Does he have the ability and the character?"

Gwyneth's heart soared as her father nodded his agreement. "Yes, he does." Then his brow lowered as he looked at Gavin. "I think he has plans beyond a knighthood—plans that include my daughter. Do you remember, Gavin, that I told you I would forgive and forget your past unless you stole from me? I have come to believe you have stolen my daughter's heart."

Gavin's stomach knotted and he was afraid to look at Gwyneth. "My lord, it's true that I care a great deal for your daughter—"

"And I for him," Gwyneth staunchly interrupted.

"Let him finish, child," her father commanded, and she meekly obeyed.

That didn't fill Gavin with confidence, yet he continued. Given what he hoped, and given that he had vowed to become an honest man, he would tell the truth. "I hope someday to prove worthy of your daughter's hand in marriage."

The earl's expression didn't change. "You do, eh? You, a thief, think I will let you even dare to consider marrying my daughter?"

Gavin desperately looked to Sir Henry, who stared down at his fingernails as if he had suddenly decided they needed trimming.

Gavin swallowed and got to his feet. "Yes, my lord, I do dare, because Gwyneth told me that she would dare to consider it, too."

She rose and took his hand. "He's right, Father. Nothing would make me happier."

"Nothing?" the earl demanded, his brow lowering. "Nothing at all?"

"No."

He stood and went toward them, every inch the Norman nobleman.

And then a warm smile blossomed on his face. "Then I think I have little to do except to say that I hope he can earn an knighthood, too. If he does, you have my blessing to wed."

He held out his arms and Gwyneth fell into his embrace. Gavin let out his breath slowly, happy beyond words, almost afraid to think he had heard correctly.

"You know," Sir Henry began as he continued to contemplate his impeccable fingernails, "I am in need of a squire. And so is my younger brother, David. It seems to me that there was a rather fierce young fellow with red hair who would do for him. I myself would rather have Gavin of Inverlea, if he will serve me."

"I would be honored!" Gavin cried, bowing. "And your brother should welcome Hollis. He's the best of the men I trained. That's no exaggeration, sir. He's very good."

"I will take your word for it," Sir Henry said with a chuckle. "And given that the king has rewarded my past glories with the estate of the discredited DeVilliers, neither of you will have to travel far to see your sweethearts—once you have finished your duties, of course."

Sir Henry gave the earl a pointed look as he got to his feet. "William, I believe we should leave the young people to discuss the future."

The earl didn't budge and his gaze flicked warily from his beaming daughter to the grinning Gavin. "I don't. They aren't going to *discuss* anything."

"Now, William, I seem to recall a certain tale concerning a barn . . ."

"Henry, you are my good friend, but if you think I'm going to walk out and leave my daughter——"

"Come along, William." Sir Henry sauntered toward the door. "I want some wine. It's been a very long day."

"Gwyneth, you could get Sir Henry some——"

"No, she can't. Come, William, or I'll knock you over the head and carry you from here."

"Well, if you're going to threaten a man," the earl muttered under his breath as he finally followed Sir Henry to the door. He paused on the threshold and looked at his daughter, then at Gavin. "I shall return in a very short time," he warned as he departed.

Gavin strode over to the door and closed it, then hurried to take Gwyneth's hands in his. He spun her around. "Can you believe it? I am to be a squire after all!"

"Of course I can," she laughed, giddy and dizzy with happiness as well as the spinning. "You will be the best squire in England. I knew you could be the moment I saw you in the wood."

"Liar," he teased as he stopped and drew her into his embrace. "I was nothing but a thief when you saw me in the wood."

She shook her head, suddenly serious. "No, you weren't. You were always better than that, Gavin. I saw it, the men saw it, my father saw it, and Sir Henry did, too.

Whatever happens, it is because of what is inside you."

He caressed her cheek. "Right now, I am full of love for you. If I succeed, that will be why."

She held him close, loving him with all her heart. "I'm so happy! I don't think anybody in England could be happier than I am."

"Hollis may be, when he hears what Sir Henry has suggested."

"And Semeli, too, perhaps."

With a brilliant smile, she lifted her face to press a tender kiss upon his lips. "But I doubt it."

DEAR READER:

Who doesn't love a bad boy? And Gavin is the best kind—a bad boy with a good heart. No wonder Gwyneth can't resist him!

Sometimes it can go the other way, though: a guy who seems like the perfect hero turns out not to be so great after all. In the next Avon True Romance, Meg Cabot's NICOLA AND THE VISCOUNT, the dashing Sebastian Bartholomew is everything Nicola Sparks thinks she wants in a husband. That is, until the infuriating Nathaniel Sheridan begins to cast doubt on the viscount's character. Will Nicola figure out Lord Sebastian is not all she thinks he is in time to break it off with him? And why does Nathaniel care so much?

Read on for a sneak peek at the latest from the author of THE PRINCESS DIARIES . . .

Abby McAden
Editor, Avon True Romance

FROM
NICOLA AND THE VISCOUNT
by Meg Cabot

Dear Nana,

> *I hope you received the gifts I sent you. The shawl is pure Chinese silk, and the pipe I sent for Puddy is ivory-handled! You needn't worry about the expense; I was able to use my monthly stipend. I am staying with the Bartholomews—I told you about them in my last letter—and they won't let me spend a penny on myself! Lord Farelly insists on paying for everything. He is such a kind man. He is very interested in locomotives and the railway. He says that someday, all of England will be connected by rail, and that one might start out in the morning in Brighton, and at the end of the day find oneself in Edinburgh!*

> *I found that a bit hard to believe, as I'm certain you do, too, but that is what he says.*

Nicola paused in her letter writing to read over what she had already written. As she did so, she nibbled thoughtfully on the feathered end of her pen.

Nana was not, of course, her real grandmother. Nicola

had no real grandparents, all of them having been carried away by influenza before she was even born. Because her sole remaining relative, Lord Renshaw, had had no interest in nor knowledge of raising a little girl, Nicola had been reared, until she was old enough to go away to school, by the wife of the caretaker of her father's estate, Beckwell Abbey. It was to this woman—and her husband, whom Nicola affectionately referred to as Puddy—that Nicola looked for grandmotherly advice and comfort. Dependent, as Nicola was, on the small income the local farmers supplied by renting the abbey's many rolling fields for their sheep to graze upon, Nana and Puddy lived modestly, but well.

But never so well as Nicola had been living for the past month. The Bartholomews, as it turned out, were every bit as wealthy as Phillip Sheridan had declared . . . perhaps even wealthier.

But what Phillip had not mentioned, since he could not have known, was that the Bartholomews were also generous, almost to a fault. Nicola needed to express only the slightest desire, and her wish was immediately granted. She had learned to bite back exclamations over bonnets or trinkets at the many shops she and Honoria frequented, lest she find herself the owner of whatever it was she'd admired. She could not allow these kind people to keep buying gifts for her . . . especially as she had no way to return the favor.

Besides which, Nicola did not really *need* new gowns or

bonnets. Necessity, in the form of her limited income, had forced her to become a skilled and creative seamstress. She had taught herself how to alter an old gown with a new flounce or sleeves until it looked as if it had just come straight from a Parisian dress shop. And she was almost as fine a milliner as any in the city, having rendered many an out-of-fashion bonnet stylish in the extreme with an artful addition of a silk rose here, or an artificial cherry there.

Eyeing her letter, Nicola wondered if she ought to add something about the God. It seemed as if it might be a good idea, since it was entirely possible that Sebastian Bartholomew was going to play an important role in all of their lives, if things kept up the way they had been. Having grown up almost completely sheltered from them, Nicola knew very little, it was true, about young men, but it did seem to her that Honoria's brother had been *most* attentive since she'd come to stay. He escorted the girls nearly every where they went, except when he was not busy with his own friends, who were quite fond of gambling and horses, like most young men—except perhaps Nathaniel Sheridan, who was too concerned with managing his father's many estates ever to stop for a game of whist or bagatelle.

Even more exciting, the God was always the first to ask Nicola for a dance at whatever ball they happened to be attending. Sometimes he even secured *two* dances with her in a single evening. Three dances with a gentlemen to whom she was not engaged, of course, would be scandalous, so that was not even a possibility.

On these occasions, of course, Nicola's heart sang, and she could not believe there existed in London a happier soul than she. It seemed incredible, but it appeared she had actually accomplished what she'd set out to do, which was impress the young Viscount Farnsworth—for that was Lord Sebastian's title, which he would hold until his father died, and he assumed the title of Earl of Farelly—with her wit and charm. How she had done it—and quite without the help of any face powder—she could not say, but she did not think she could be mistaken in the signs: the God admired her, at least a little. She supposed her hair, which she wore upswept all the time now, with Martine's aid, had helped.

All that Nicola needed to forever seal her happiness was for the God to propose marriage. If he did—no, when, *when*—she had already decided she would say yes.

But there was, in the back of her mind, a niggling doubt that such a proposal might ever really materialize. She was, after all, not wealthy. She had nothing but her passably pretty face and keen fashion sense to recommend her. Handsome young men of wealth and importance rarely asked penniless girls like Nicola—even penniless girls of good family and excellent education—to marry them. Love matches were all well and good, but, as Madame had often reminded them, starvation is not pleasant. Young men who did not marry as their fathers instructed them often found themselves cut off without a cent. And it was perfectly untrue that one could live on love alone. Love could not, after all, put bread on the table and meat in the larder.

But from parental objections to a match between her and the God, at least, Nicola felt she was safe. Lord and Lady Farelly seemed prodigiously fond of her. Why, in the short time since she'd come to live with them, they seemed already to think of her as a second daughter, including her in all of their family conversations, and even occasionally dropping their formal address of her as Miss Sparks, and calling her Nicola.

No, should Lord Sebastian see fit to propose to her, she could foresee no difficulties from *that* quarter. But would he? Would he propose to a girl who was merely pretty but not beautiful? A girl with freckles on her nose, who had only recently been allowed to put her hair up? An orphan with only a bit of property in Northumberland and a vast knowledge of the romantic poets?

He had to. He just *had* to! Nicola felt it as surely as she felt that the color ochre on a redheaded woman was an abomination.